Other books by Patricia K. Azeltine:

We Meet Again . . .
Temporary Husband
The Marriage Scheme

TRACES OF LOVE

TRACES OF LOVE

•

Patricia K. Azeltine

AVALON BOOKS
NEW YORK

Published by Thomas Bouregy & Co., Inc.
160 Madison Avenue, New York, NY 10016

Library of Congress Cataloging-in-Publication Data

Azeltine, Patricia K.
Traces of love / Patricia K. Azeltine.
p. cm.
Novel.
ISBN 0-8034-9777-6 (acid-free paper)
I. Title.

PS3551.A94T76 2006
813'.6—dc22

2005037652

PRINTED IN THE UNITED STATES OF AMERICA
ON ACID-FREE PAPER
BY HADDON CRAFTSMEN, BLOOMSBURG, PENNSYLVANIA

To Steve, Mary, Katie, Jean, Bonneville,
Terry and Jessica.

"A real friend is one who walks in when the rest
of the world walks out."—Walter Winchell

Chapter One

A spine-prickling sensation came over Melissa Douglas as she ran down Cass Street, heading for her uncle's general store. She glanced over her shoulder, seeing no one around, and yet, she had the strangest feeling something was terribly wrong. Brushing the notion off, she continued on, careful not to slip on the slick wooden boards that made up most of Astoria's developed streets.

The store, like most of the businesses in town, was built on piers and housed a damp musty odor. Water from the Columbia River rushed below the piles and could be seen just by looking through the gaps between the boards.

Wind whipped the rain against the weather-worn walls and on its cedar shingled roof. Missy shivered, the cold and wet seeping through her cloak and into her layers of clothing. She had yet to adapt to the rainy coastal weather.

Why had she ever come to Astoria, Oregon?

Unfortunately, she knew the answer to that question. Her father had insisted she move to Astoria to live with her Uncle Irvine, so she could be closer to her betrothed, Surgeon Richard Barnes, her father's protégé, who worked at the Vancouver Barracks on the other side of the Columbia River across from the bustling city of Portland and located a day's boat ride from Astoria. Little did she know that in only two months of living out West, she would break off her engagement. Her father had been so furious with her that she hadn't returned home. Instead, she remained in Astoria, helping her uncle run his general store.

The door, slightly askew, creaked as she opened it. She slipped into the dark interior of the store. The only light came from windows too dirty to see through and a lantern hanging on a peg on the wall behind the counter. Missy glanced around. Haunting shadows lurked in every recess.

The nagging feeling crept into her gut again. Something was wrong. Her uncle had never asked her to come to the store so late in the evening before. "Uncle Irvine, I have a message that you wanted to see me." She lowered the hood of her wet coat. Seeing no sign of her uncle, she sidled around a table of goods.

Angry voices echoed from the back of the store. Missy recognized her uncle's voice. Surprised by the hatred that spewed forth in his tone, she listened. Scooting against the side wall, she could see her uncle conversing with Devlin McCoy, a prominent and powerful citizen of Astoria. Devlin McCoy had made a fortune investing in banking and real estate, but his ambitions ran far beyond that. His sights were set on becoming senator of Oregon. What business could McCoy have with her uncle? He had never set foot in her uncle's little store before and had never even acknowledged either of them on the street or at church.

Despite being a distinguished-looking man, Devlin McCoy always made Missy feel uneasy. His well-groomed peppered hair and mustache complemented his deep brown eyes. He carried his slender six-foot frame well and could always be seen wearing a fine tailored suit. In church, Missy had noticed he had a habit of glancing at his gold pocket watch that had *DM* engraved on its cover.

"Where'd you hide those documents?" Devlin demanded.

"I'll never tell you—you Confederate slime," Irvine spat each word out. "Took me years to gather that information. But it'll be worth it if it puts you behind bars. Or better yet, gets you hung by your scrawny neck."

Devlin grabbed Irvine by the shirt and shook him. "I'll kill you before you ever get a word to anyone about my past."

Irvine wobbled on his one leg, jabbing his cane on the floor, desperate to regain his balance.

Devlin released his hold as if touching Irvine repulsed him.

Hopping over to his desk, Irvine turned, then leaned against the sturdy wood furniture. "You see, it was your men who left me like this. Most of your soldiers went back over the bodies, dead and wounded, and robbed them of any valuables they had. And then you and your men raided towns all over Ohio, Kentucky, and Indiana."

Shrugging, Devlin said, "It was war. Why shouldn't we have profited from it? Other's had."

Irvine shook his head. "We don't need men like you shaping our government. And I won't let it happen. I'll let the world know that Colonel James Huge Morgan never died, but escaped out West and took on the identity of Devlin McCoy. Was that the name of the dead Union soldier you changed clothes with?"

Devlin drew an ivory-handled knife, one with a long and forbidding blade. The blade metal flashed when the light caught it just right. Missy gasped, but neither man heard her.

"You know much more than I would have given you credit for. But it's all for naught." He pointed the knife at Irvine and said, "Give me the documents you have and I'll let you live. Otherwise you're a dead man."

"It doesn't matter if you kill me or not. The truth will come out in the end. I've made sure of that," Irvine said.

"And what about that niece of yours?"

Irvine drew his bushy gray brows together. "You leave her out of this. She knows nothing."

Devlin rubbed the side of the blade against his cleanly shaven jaw. "One of my favorite things to do to a Yank was stab him in the gut and twist the knife. I'd listen to him squeal like a pig. It'll be a pleasure doing that to you." In one stride, Devlin towered over Irvine. With a mighty thrust, he plunged his knife just below Irvine's sternum and cranked it clockwise. Irvine released a deep-throated grunt before his body collapsed to the ground.

Missy stared in shock. Her head hit the wall as she covered her mouth with one hand to muzzle a scream. Too frozen to move, she could only listen to Devlin let out a wicked laugh before he dashed from the store.

When the door slammed shut Missy snapped back to reality. She rushed around the counter and crouched down next to her uncle. Irvine lay in a pool of blood. Rolling his body over, she gazed at him. Crimson stained his white shirt. Missy held his hand in hers and felt a faint squeeze.

Irvine's eyes slit open and his lips parted.

A lump formed in Missy's throat. She could hardly breathe let alone talk, but she forced the words out. "Uncle Irvine, what's happening? Why'd he—"

"Get out of Astoria," Irvine murmured. A gurgling in his throat accompanied his cough. "Take the money and key." He gasped for a breath. "Get out of town."

"You'll be fine, Uncle Irvine." Her trembling voice betrayed her words. "I'll get a doctor." Her hands shook as she reached for the knife. His words stopped her before she could touch the deadly metal.

"You're in danger. The money box. The key—" Irvine took a quick breath, then expired.

"No!" Missy cried. "Uncle Irvine." Missy's voice cracked as a sob burst forth. "Wake up. Please. You'll be fine." She buried her face in her hands, her body shaking uncontrollably. Hugging herself, she murmured, "I don't understand any of this."

The door to the front of the store creaked open. Missy felt a cool gust of air filter through the room. A shiver shot down her spine. She stared at the money box sitting on the desk. Quietly, she reached out, slid the box off and set it on the floor. Opening the lid, she snatched the money and key from inside and shoved them in her walking boot. Then she slipped the box under the desk, hoping the shadows would be enough to hide it. She waited.

Still wearing a long black overcoat and beaver-skin hat, Devlin McCoy stood before her. Blood was splattered on his coat and shoes.

"You did this," she whispered, forcing herself to look at the man. Standing up, she held her head high, her shoulders back, and spine stiff. Clutching the folds of her dress, she hid her shaking hands.

He smiled derisively, then strode toward her. Reaching out, he turned her head to one side, and then the other. "No. He did this," Devlin said. He dropped his hand to his side. "Your uncle should have listened to me. Unfortunately, you're going to pay the price. What a waste . . ." He made clicking noises with his tongue. "A woman of your beauty. Rare, indeed."

He moved only a few feet away. "I didn't even know you were here until I was heading out the door. I caught a whiff of your perfume. Expensive. Seductive. French. I smelled it on you before and liked it."

Missy glared at him. "If you wanted his store you could have bought it. Why kill him for it?"

Devlin laughed. Sobering quickly, he studied her before speaking. "You really don't know, do you?"

"Know what?"

"Your uncle got involved in my personal business. I didn't like it."

"Did he owe you money?"

He ignored her question. "Hmm. Now what am I supposed to do with you?" He sighed. "I can't let you go. You know I killed your uncle. I can't trust you not to tell the marshal, the man never did like me." He crossed his arms over his chest and drummed his fingers. "I guess I'll have to accuse you of the murder."

"Why would I murder my uncle?"

"Money." He moved closer to her and ran his finger across her throat. "What a shame this delicate neck will be snapped by a rope when they hang you for murder. Don't worry, my dear, it'll be over quickly."

Missy jerked away from his touch. "You're an evil man," she said in a whisper.

His eyes darkened to an even deeper brown, looking almost like two black balls. "You don't know the meaning of evil unless you've served in the war. You Yankees are the evil ones, killing my men down as if they were nothing more than wild dogs, and torturing them in those disgusting prisons."

"My father and mother healed both Union and Confederate soldiers, and they were proud of it. The war has been over for years." She frowned. "None of this conversation makes any sense. What does this have to do with my uncle?"

"I've said all I'm going to say on the matter. Besides, you have other things to worry about, like preparing for your hanging." A deep-throated laugh rumbled from his chest as if he found hangings entertaining.

"You can't prove a lie in court. The truth always comes out," Missy said.

Devlin stepped over Irvine's body as if he was nothing more than a sack of flour, and then whirled around to look at her. An arrogant grin formed on his mouth. "I can and I will. I'm an important man in this community. Who's going to believe you over me?"

"I received a message from my uncle to come here immediately. People at the boardinghouse saw it." Missy glared at Devlin, wanting desperately to punch his long thin nose off his face and strangle him with his graying handlebar mustache.

"That proves you were here," Devlin said, grinning.

Missy tilted her head and glared at him defiantly. "Well, if I'm going to be convicted of killing a man, why not make it two in one night and kill you as well?"

Devlin laughed. "I like your spirit. Could have used you in the war." Placing his foot on Irving's chest, Devlin reached out and yanked the knife free, wiping the blood off on the victim's pants. "Morty. Moose."

Two men Missy had seen in Devlin's company on a few occasions came forward. Only the counter separated them from Missy. Moose's head seemed out of proportion to his hulking size and weight. His shape reminded Missy of the sea lions that lounged about on the rocks. Morty was just the opposite with a large head and thin body. They both wore sailors' garb and smelled like a mixture of fish and whiskey.

Devlin never took his eyes off of Missy as he spoke. "Escort Miss Douglas to jail. Report this murder to the marshal. Tell him I saw Missy Douglas kill her uncle in cold blood."

"You'll never get away with this," Missy said through gritted teeth.

Again, Devlin laughed. Moose came around the

counter and roughly seized Missy by the arm. When they reached the middle of the store Morty clamped on to her other arm, and they both dragged her to the front of the store.

Moose kicked the door open and was greeted by pounding rain. Gray clouds darkened the sky, making the time of day appear more like midnight rather than early evening. Morty released hold of her while he grabbed for a lantern that hung on a peg near the door.

While Moose wasn't looking, Missy lifted her hand to her neck and carefully unbuttoned her coat, her mind whirling with ideas of escape.

"What's taking you so long?" Moose asked, an edge in his voice.

"The winds blowin' so hard I can't light the damn thing," Morty said. Blocking the wind with his back, he struck a match and lit the wick, and then clamped the glass over the flame. "There." Whirling around, he handed it to Moose. "Come on. Let's get out of this rain."

Having strolled, run, and even skipped this pier many times during the last year, Missy knew every crack, slippery spot, loose board, and worn-out planks in it. She kept her stare at the approaching corner, where the pier took a sharp right. In the past, she had come close to falling in the water at this very spot many times.

Missy began to slip her right arm out of the sleeve. Just as they reached the corner, Morty hit a slick patch and wavered. At that very second, Missy whipped open her coat and slid out of it. Moose tottered, struggling to gain his balance. Seizing the opportunity, Missy pushed Moose into the water. Moose yelped before he splashed into the river.

Whirling around, she sprinted down the pier. Morty pursued her. Quickly she approached a bridge. The darkness gave her an advantage and she made good use of it as she darted left. Her foot slipped slightly, but she hastily recovered. As she reached another sharp right, she halted and frantically searched the area for a place to hide. Two barrels lurked in the shadows of a business building entrance. Darting behind one, she waited.

Morty ran full speed in her direction. As he approached her Missy stuck her leg out. Morty tripped, crying out as he plunged into the icy waters below.

Missy rubbed her ankle where Morty had collided into her. She would surely have a bruise by tomorrow. Lifting her skirt, she jogged the rest of the way, not stopping until she reached Mrs. Baker's boardinghouse on Jefferson Street.

Now what? She couldn't let Mrs. Baker see her. The less her landlady knew the better chance the older woman had of staying alive. Missy owed Mrs. Baker that much. Mrs. Baker had been like a mother to her since she had moved to Astoria.

Rounding the house, she cracked open the back door. A few lights were on and she heard murmurs in the parlor. She held her breath as she moved up the back stairs, cringing each time she heard a step creak. Once in her room, she released a sigh of relief.

With no time to lose, she packed only a few items of

clothing, a hair brush, and what little money she had into a small bag. She put on another wool coat and wished she had had enough time to change into drier clothes. Returning down the stairs, she crept back outside.

Chapter Two

Now came the hard part: How to get out of town without being seen. She could board a passenger steamer, but that would be the first place McCoy would look for her. The stagecoaches and trains didn't run until morning, and both would be easy for Devlin to find her on.

She had to think. A swaying light on a boat at the port caught her eye. That was it! She would stow away on a boat heading for Portland, and she knew just the boat that would take her there. The *Fannie Mae*, a stern-wheeler steamboat that carried mail between Portland and Astoria, left from Flavel's wharf daily in the early morning hours, usually no later than six.

Scurrying along the pier, Missy kept herself well hidden in the recesses of buildings. Where no business buildings stood farther out on the piers, she resorted to using empty crates and exposed pilings to hide herself. She noticed the *Fannie Mae*'s gangway was still out. Lady luck was smiling on her tonight. The captain and crew must have gone into town, which meant only a few seamen would be aboard.

She tiptoed up the gangway and onboard the ship, searching desperately for a place to hide. Missy climbed down into the bowels of the ship where it had been filled with cargo. She found several barrels bunched together, where she hunkered down and waited. Missy dozed off and on, waking once when the crew returned from their night in town, and again when the ship's engines roared to life in the morning. She shivered uncontrollably from cold and fear. At long last, the paddle wheels churned and the boat pulled away from the dock.

The trip took ten hours with the steamboat stopping at Knappa, Clifton, West Port, Kalama, and St. Helens, arriving in Portland around four in the afternoon. Missy's muscles felt stiff and sore, her legs cramped. She wondered if she could even walk after so many hours of being huddled in the same position.

Peeking around a barrel, she waited for the paddle wheel to cease moving, the boat to be tied up to the dock, and the gangway set out. They would unload immediately, so she would have to time her escape just right. If she got caught she would be in even more trouble than she was at the moment.

Her heart hammered in her chest as she tiptoed up the stairs. A passenger steamboat had just unloaded next to the *Fannie Mae*, making the docks busy with people. Missy tried her best to remain calm as she padded over to the gangway, her bag in hand.

She treaded down, and had almost made it to the dock when she heard a man's voice yell, "Hey lady.

What are you doing on board this boat?" Missy froze, and the man yelled, "Stowaway!"

Missy sprinted off the rest of the gangway. Pushing and shoving, she scampered through the throng of people. She wasn't even sure if someone was after her until she reached Front Street and glanced over her shoulder. Two men from the steamboat pursued her.

Holding her breath, she raced down the street. She gasped for air, her lungs burning. Fear caused her stomach to clench into a painful knot. She whizzed by many buildings, most of which were clapboard and two-story.

The men were closing in on her. Where could she go? Suppressing her panic, she scanned the area for a hiding place. With no time to waste, she scampered into an alley and, panting, braced her back against the wall of a building. Watching the opening of the alley, she saw one man streak by. Briefly she closed her eyes, relieved. She had lost them.

Jacob Gilbert strolled down Front Street, heading for Harvey's General Store. He had a list of supplies he needed to buy and haul up to his cabin on Mt. Hood. The rain had finally stopped, leaving the air with a fresh, clean odor of pine resin. He loved that smell. He started to whistle a tune when he suddenly stopped. A woman, who looked the spitting image of his former fiancée ran toward him. He rubbed his eyes. When he gazed again, she skedaddled down an alley. Was that Rachael? But that was impossible. Rachael was dead. Murdered.

Jogging down the boardwalk, Jake scooted around groups of people strolling up and down the boardwalk and searched each alleyway, looking for the dark-haired beauty. Reaching the second alley, he halted, spotting the woman being accosted by two burly men.

As he approached them he took a closer look at her. His heart just about stopped beating. Amazing. She could have been Rachael's twin.

A feeling of elation rushed through him, followed by confusion. Rachael had died in his arms. He had felt the life force dwindle from her delicate body. So how could this woman be her?

The need to protect her surged through him. He had not been able to save Rachael. He wouldn't make that mistake twice. "What's going on here?" Jake asked.

"This woman's a stowaway," the seaman said.

"Is this true?" Jake asked.

The woman hesitated. "No. They're mistaken." She appeared frightened and confused.

"Release her," Jake demanded.

"But—" one of the men protested.

"But nothing. I said release her," Jake said.

The man holding her said, "And who's going to make us?"

Calmly, Jake said, "I am."

The bigger of the two men stepped forward and threw a clumsy swing. Jake counterpunched to the man's mid-section. He doubled over, groaning and fell to his knees. The second man, much smaller, decided not to press the issue. Instead he rushed over to his friend and helped him up. "You're making a big mistake," he said to Jake.

Jake waited for the two men to hurry away before he approached Rachael's lookalike. "Are you all right?"

"Yes," she said breathlessly. "Thank you." For the

first time she got a good look at this stranger. He had thick dark brown hair, which looked as if it had been cut recently. She could see the intelligence in his blue eyes—a man who missed very little. His jaw spoke of a determined will, and the smooth lines of his clean shaven face gave him an aristocratic appearance. Yet he wore a buckskin rifleman's coat, a coontail cap, denim trousers, and leather upper mucking boots. He looked to be a contrast of a gentleman and a mountain man.

"I'm Jacob Gilbert. My friends call me Jake." His eyes seemed to look right through her. He extended his hand.

She shook his hand and said, "I'm Melissa Douglas." Missy felt a flutter in her stomach the second she touched Jake's hand. A warmth spread to her limbs, along with heat rising to her face. She fumbled with the latch on her bag. "I feel I should pay you for your assistance."

He looked offended. "I would never accept, Miss Douglas—"

"Missy. Please. Call me Missy."

"Where are you staying, Missy?"

She liked the deep baritone of his voice, so soothing, so manly. "I . . . uh . . . I'm . . . uh . . ." Why was she so tongue-tied? Why was her heart thudding in her chest like beating drums every time she merely gazed at him? She released a breath that she didn't realized she had been holding. "I don't even know. I'm new in town. I've only been to Portland once before, so I don't really know my way around."

"May I recommend the Palace Hotel?" Jake said.

Missy had heard of the Palace Hotel where only the

very rich stayed while visiting Portland. "That sounds beyond my means," Missy said.

When he grinned, his eyes sparkled like finely shined gems. "No problem. I know the owner. I'll make sure he's fair."

For the first time in a long time, Missy felt comforted. In turn, she flashed him one of her warmest smiles. "Then, kind sir, lead the way."

He crooked his arm for her to grab hold of and carried her bag in his other hand. At a leisurely pace, they strolled to the more upscale part of Portland, which boasted a theater and large post office building. Once at the hotel, Jake held the door open for Missy and followed her inside. Then he escorted her to the front desk.

Missy gazed around in awe. Everything in this hotel spoke of elegance, from the red velvet upholstered settee's to the enormous decorative crystal chandelier that hung in the lobby. A feeling of alarm raced through her. How would she afford such a place?

"Simon," Jake said to the clerk at the front desk.

"Back so soon?" Simon said. His gaze drifted to Missy. "Well now, who do we have here?"

"This is Miss Douglas. She needs a room. I told her I know the owner and that he would give her a room for a reasonable price."

Simon gave Jake a lopsided grin. "Okay. How does room two-twenty sound?"

"Just fine." Jake accompanied Missy up the stairs and directed her to her room. "If I may be so bold—" Now it was Jake's turn to get tongue-tied. He hesitated. "I was wondering if maybe, if you weren't busy that is . . ." Red seeped into his perfectly handsome face.

Missy decided to make it easy on him and asked, "Are you asking me to supper?"

Jake sighed. "Yes. But I'm not doing a very good job of it, am I?"

Missy smiled. "I think you're doing a wonderful job of it."

"Well, would you like to accompany me to supper this evening?"

"I don't have much to wear," she said, taking her bag from his hands.

"What you have on is just fine." He rushed on, "I know of a good family restaurant just a few doors down." When she didn't answer he asked, "How does seven sound?"

Missy tried to suppress her stomach from growling. She hadn't eaten from the evening before, not having had anything on the long boat ride. With very little money to her name, and not sure how she would pay for her hotel room, a free meal sounded pretty darn good right now. "I'll meet you in the lobby."

Jake's smile widened, displaying his straight white teeth. This man took very good care of himself, despite his rugged attire. "Looking forward to it."

She watched him stroll down the hall. The back view of him was just as impressive as the front, his broad shoulders and strong muscular legs were easy on the eyes. As soon as he disappeared from sight she returned to the sanctuary of her room. What had she just done? She's wanted for murder and she's letting a man court her in town. Worse yet, she gave him her real name! By now every lawman in town was probably looking for her. How stupid could she be?

Her stomach growled, reminding her just how hungry she was. She would have dinner with Jake, and then get on about her business. Trudging to the bed, she felt weak and tired. She pulled out her money and counted it. After she paid for the hotel room she wouldn't have enough for a train or stage ticket. Nor could she rent a horse. She needed a job. If she was lucky, Marshal Tanner would give her time. Maybe she should have gone to him and told him everything.

She shook her head. No. Even though Marshal Tanner wasn't owned or controlled by anyone in town, he still had to answer to the wealthy who ran Astoria. Devlin McCoy could put a lot of pressure on the marshal as well as many others in town. He had done it before and would do it again. She couldn't do that to the marshal and his family, people she considered her friends.

She had to face facts. She was alone in this. Alone and scared.

Jake turned the corner and paused, glancing over his shoulder at a blank wall. He felt her eyes on him until he had disappeared from sight. His gut instinct told him she was lying about not being a stowaway. Normally when a person lied to him he didn't give that person a second thought. But he couldn't resist helping Missy. Even up close she looked so much like Rachael. He pulled out a photograph he kept in his shirt pocket close to his heart. Rachael stared back at him, her solemn eyes reaching into his soul, into his mind, blaming him for what had happened to her.

Nausea rose in his belly. He needed a drink. He escaped out the back of the building and headed to

Stark Street, where he entered the Gem Saloon, a popular oyster bar. He selected a table in the back where he could be alone in his thoughts. He couldn't ever escape his past, his guilt, his mistakes. God it had been eight years since she had died, died at the hands of a man *he* had gotten acquitted. Jake shook his head, not wanting to relive that painful time, those dreadful memories. He had moved from Boston to Portland in hopes of escaping that period in his life, but nothing could ever erase what he had done and to whom.

After ordering a whiskey, he sat there staring blankly across the room. Maybe he should cancel dinner with Missy. He had no right to get involved with a woman again. Hadn't the first time turned out to be a disaster? He had been run out of Boston by Rachael's socially elite family, the Hancocks. He hadn't blamed them. He had killed their daughter, just as if he had slit her throat himself.

Thomas Hancock, owner of the law firm Jake had worked for, had blackballed him from working for any other firm on the East Coast, his connections far reaching and powerful. Jake had had no choice but to get away and begin a new life. He knew that that had been the only way to save his family from having to pay the price for his mistakes. So he went as far west as possible.

Missy's emerald eyes, thick black hair, flawless skin, and full pink lips flashed in his mind. God Almighty, she was gorgeous. He had to admit she was different from Rachael. Where Rachael had been stoic, quiet, and serious, Missy seemed more full of life. He liked that. He also liked her natural beauty. Her clothes had been disheveled as if she had been sleeping in them all night. And her hair was in disarray, most of the locks falling out of the loose bun she had at the nape of her neck. Yet nothing could hide the gentle curves of her face, the allure of her eyes, and tempting shape of her mouth. She looked to be close to twenty, give or take a few years. A sharp pain stabbed at him again. That was the age Rachael had been when she was slain.

What was he doing? He knew better than to get involved, but she drew him to her like gravity held a man earthbound.

Jake sighed. He would go to dinner with Miss Douglas, and hope his curiosity would be satisfied, curbing any further need to see her, be with her, and especially, the desire to kiss her. Once he had her out of his mind, he could resume his life, shuffling between the town and the mountain, living mostly in solitary, just the way he wanted it.

Chapter Three

Jake checked his pocket watch, noting she was fifteen minutes late. Was she having second thoughts like he had earlier? He couldn't blame her and would understand if she didn't show. After all, they had just met. He was a complete stranger to her. Should he go to her room and check to see if she was running late?

No. He had too much pride for that. He would give her ten more minutes, and then return to his room on the third floor. Picking up the *Oregonian*, he leaned against the wall while he glanced at the headlines and occasionally at the people entering and exiting the lobby.

He ran a finger under the collar of his shirt and jacket. He couldn't recall the last time he had worn a suit. Had it been in Boston? Since moving to Oregon, he hadn't had a reason to wear a suit. The attire used to feel comfortable. Now it felt suffocating. He had bought it earlier in the day, just to wear to dinner with

Missy. He wasn't sure whether he put it on to impress her or because his trapper-style clothing just didn't seem appropriate.

A few minutes later, Missy descended the stairs. Jake couldn't take his eyes off of her. She wore a simple white blouse and a blue skirt, yet she would outshine any socialite dressed in fine European silk. She had combed her hair and wore it in a chignon, just as Rachael had always worn hers.

Spotting him, she smiled, causing a warmth to ignite in the pit of his stomach. He hurried to her side.

"I hardly recognized you in your black suit," Missy said. "You look like a proper gentleman."

"So before I looked like a rogue?" Jake said, teasing. He took her shawl and placed it on her shoulders.

"No. Just, um, rugged."

He crooked his elbow. He liked it when she slid her hand around his arm. They left the hotel and strolled a few blocks down to a family restaurant. "Not too fancy, but nice enough to keep the riffraff out," Jake said, holding the door open.

They were seated at an out-of-the-way table, just what Jake had requested earlier in the day. Once their wine was poured and dinner ordered, Jake leaned back in his chair. He couldn't seem to stop himself from staring at Missy.

"So where did you say you were from, Miss Douglas?" Jake asked. He took a sip of wine.

"I didn't."

"Why don't you tell me now?"

Her gaze dipped before directing it back at him. "I guess everywhere." At his questioning expression she added, "My father's a military man. We moved around."

"Is he stationed at the Vancouver Barracks?" Jake asked.

"No. I moved here because I had an uncle who lived in Astoria and I wanted to live in one place for once. I got pretty tired of military living."

"I would think a beautiful woman would never get tired of all the eligible bachelors fawning over her," Jake said.

She smiled, but never confirmed or denied his compliment. "What about you?"

Jake's spine stiffened. He couldn't meet her eyes when he said, "I suppose I moved out here because of the lure of the Wild West."

"And is it everything you had hoped it would be?"

He shrugged, gulping his wine. He quickly changed the subject back to her. "If your uncle lives in Astoria, are you visiting Portland?"

"Actually my uncle recently passed away."

"I'm sorry."

She paused before continuing. "So I came to Portland to find a job. I want to make enough money to travel back East and be with my family. The sooner I get back home the better."

Jake felt a streak of disappointment shoot through him. How could he get her to stay longer? Maybe if he found her a job, here in Portland, then she might stay longer. "What can you do?" Jake blurted out.

"Excuse me?" She frowned.

"I thought perhaps I could help you find work."

"You're awfully helpful, Mr. Gilbert. First you rescue me from seamen and now you're offering to help me find a job. Do you do this for every woman you meet in town?"

Jake put on an easy smile. "I guess you caught me."

Missy's body stiffened. "Caught you?"

"If I may be so bold as to say I find myself attracted to you." He rushed on saying, "How couldn't I? You're beautiful." He gauged her reaction, pleased when she smiled.

She hesitated, and then said, "I have a lot of experience in nursing. I'm pretty good with bookkeeping. I'm a fair cook. And I can clean houses and wash clothes."

Their meals were set before them halting the conversation. Missy immediately dug into her food, eating quickly as if she hadn't eaten in weeks.

Jake decided to follow her lead, finding himself pretty hungry. After a long lull in the conversation Jake asked, "Do you have any brothers or sister?"

"I have a brother, Daniel." She beamed. "He's in medical school at Princeton. He's top in his class."

"Impressive."

She paused as if to assess his sincerity. She took a bite of her steak and chewed. Every movement of her face only seemed to enhance her beauty. At long last she said, "And you?"

"I have two sisters and two brothers. My sisters are married and my brothers are in a law practice together."

"Do they live out here?" Missy asked.

"No. They all live in Boston or thereabouts."

"You must miss them," she said.

"A little." Uncomfortable with the topic, Jake decided to consume more of his meal.

"So tell me what do you do for a living, Mr. Gilbert."

"I'm a tracker. I learned from the Indians how to track animals and from there I learned about tracking people."

"You're a bounty hunter?" A look of alarm crossed her face.

"Not really. I prefer to track animals that are killing livestock or people lost in the wilderness. But I have been known to track down outlaws." He studied her, and then asked, "Does that bother you?"

She shrugged. "No." Her answer came out quick and stiff. She didn't fool him. His being a tracker bothered her.

Jake wondered why, but decided not to make an issue of it at the moment.

"I think I remember reading about you in the *Oregonian* newspaper. Didn't you find that boy lost on Mt. Hood a few months back? And you found that outlaw who was robbing the stagecoach." She continued before he could answer. "I think most people would consider you a hero."

"I wouldn't go that far." Jake felt uncomfortable with her praise. He'd done his job and that was that. He refrained from telling her that he owned shares in mines and other businesses in town, one of those businesses being the Palace Hotel. The less people knew about him the better. He liked it that way. Jake finished his meal before he spoke up again. This time, he kept to more neutral subjects like the weather, the area, and local events. After dinner, they strolled back to the hotel.

As they entered the lobby, Simon, still hard at work

at the front desk said, "Mr. Gilbert. A telegram arrived for you."

Jake and Missy waited while Simon retrieved it. Instead of reading it right away, Jake shoved the telegram in his coat pocket and returned to her side. He didn't want the evening to end. He enjoyed her company, more than anyone else's in a long time.

"May I walk you to your room?" he asked.

She nodded. Little was exchanged between them on the way to her room. When they reached her door, she paused and made no attempt to open it, making it quite clear to Jake she had no intention of letting him step foot inside her room.

He hadn't courted a woman in so long that he couldn't recall the propriety for saying good night. Should he kiss her hand, her lips, bow, or just say good night and leave? Once a refined gentleman and top lawyer, now he was reduced to a boorish woodsman who dabbled in investments.

Jake held her hand, not wanting to let it go. "I enjoyed your company tonight."

"Thank you for dinner."

"May I call on you again?" Jake's heart pounded in his chest. He marveled that anyone could resurrect his shattered heart and make him feel alive again.

"I would like that. Although I can't tell you where I'll be. I can't stay in this hotel for very long."

"Stay as long as you'd like."

"As I said, I don't have much money. Hopefully I'll find a job."

"Oh, that reminds me. I have a friend who runs a boardinghouse on the outskirts of town. She's looking for someone to cook and clean for her and her boarders. Her name is Mrs. Katherine O'Sullivan. Tell her I sent you," Jake said.

Missy laid her free hand over his. "Thank you. I don't know how I'll ever repay you for your kindness. I've never met anyone like you before, so willing to help another person."

He barely heard her words. Staring at her hand, he was immensely aware of the jolt her touch gave him. He wanted to kiss her, and wanted to badly. But at the moment, he wasn't willing to risk scaring her away. He returned his gaze to her face and said, "No need to. Unless—"

"Unless what?" She grinned.

"You'd agree to dine with me again. Tomorrow morning?" Suddenly he couldn't wait until morning.

She removed both of her hands. "I would like to, but I want to see about that job."

"I'll go with you after we eat. Mrs. O'Sullivan is a dear friend of mine."

"Well . . . if you're sure."

"Positive." Jake didn't tell her he owned the building and business, and he wouldn't either. If she worked in one of his establishments, he would have a legitimate reason to see her, and see her often. Reluctantly, he said good night without kissing her and returned to his room.

So much for getting Missy Douglas out of his life. Instead of quenching his thirst for her, he felt more parched than before and only wanted to see her even more. He removed his jacket, loosened his tie, and poured himself a brandy. He took a long sip before pulling out the telegram. Reclining on the bed and propping a hand beneath his head, Jake read the short message: *Request your presence in Astoria. Immediately. Your services needed. Devlin McCoy.*

He sighed. Jake considered Devlin a good friend, but the man's timing stunk. Damn. He didn't want to go. Not now. No matter what services the man needed. Missy might be gone by the time he returned. What if he never saw her again? He looked at the piece of paper. Now he couldn't even see her tomorrow morning. Jake released another frustrated sigh. He pulled out his watch and checked the time. 9:45 P.M. Too late to catch a steamer tonight. The next one left at six in the morning. He would leave a message for Missy at the front desk apologizing for his absence and have a meal sent up to her room. Well, he hoped there would be other opportunities to meet with Missy when he returned. He knew one thing though. He would be counting the minutes down before he would see her again.

Missy stared at the freshly painted white structure, surprised at its size and how well maintained it looked. Quite a difference from the weather-worn walls of the boardinghouse she had rented in Astoria. She sucked in a deep breath and exhaled slowly before approaching the front door and strolling into the house. She needed this job so she could save enough money to get home. With her parents traveling around as much as they did, she had thought about sending them a telegram, but decided not to. It could sit in their home for weeks or months. Then she thought of her brother. Again, she decided not to send him one either. He was at a critical stage in his education and couldn't afford to come out West to help her. No. She had to do this on her own.

The inside looked like a normal boardinghouse with a parlor, dining room, and large kitchen, with many small bedrooms upstairs.

"Hello," Missy called.

An older matronly woman appeared, wearing a brown dress and white apron. Her gray hair and wrinkles around her eyes spoke of her mature age. She was short and stocky, and had a kind face and light blue eyes. "May I help you?"

"Are you Mrs. O'Sullivan?" Missy asked.

The woman nodded.

"My name is Melissa Douglas. I'm looking for a job. Mr. Gilbert suggested I check here."

"Do you have any experience cooking and cleaning?" Mrs. O'Sullivan asked. "Because the last one Mr. Gilbert sent over here had more of a notion to be waited on rather than helpin' out."

"I cook and clean and I'm a hard worker," Missy said.

"How soon can you start?"

Missy adjusted her bag to the other hand. "Now."

"Good. I could use the help. I'm behind on everything. You can have the bedroom just off the kitchen. Right now we have five tenants. We serve three meals a day, one at seven in the morning, one at noon, and another at six in the evening." She led the way into the kitchen.

Missy set her bag by the back door, took off her coat, and rolled up her sleeves. Padding over to the sink, she plunged her hands into the hot soapy water and commenced finishing up the dishes.

Missy worked quickly and thoroughly. Her father would allow nothing less in his hospital or his home.

Mrs. O'Sullivan picked up one of the plates and inspected it carefully. A smile spread on her lips, but she said nothing as she dried it, and put it away.

"When you're finished here, get settled in your room. After that, I'll need the beds made, firewood brought in, and the stoves stoked."

"And after that?" Missy asked.

"After that we start on the next meal." Mrs. O'Sullivan grinned. "I think we're going to get along just fine, Melissa. I can see why Mr. Gilbert wanted me to hire you. He finally picked a good one."

"Call me Missy." She returned the grin before she went about her chores. Despite her father being one of the top physicians and surgeons in the military, he never allowed either of his children, or his wife, to be pampered. They had been raised to work hard, efficiently, and always finish any job they started.

Missy waited until she had completed all her chores before she entered her room and placed what few items she carried with her in the dresser drawers. She filled her pitcher with water so she would have it ready when she retired this evening.

As they cooked the noon and evening meals together, she and Mrs. O'Sullivan talked about each others' pasts and the latest gossip in Portland. Mrs. O'Sullivan appeared genuinely happy to have Missy there to chat with and help with the chores.

One subject Missy stayed away from was Jake Gilbert. The older woman only volunteered that she had known him for years, but nothing more. One thing that kept rolling through Missy's mind, though, was Mrs. O'Sullivan's comment about Jake sending another woman over here before her. Just how many women had Jake sent over here? Was he some kind of fancy man who collected women? Had she misjudged him that badly? She hoped not, because she was really starting to like him.

Chapter Four

Jake waited in the parlor of Devlin McCoy's elegant Victorian Queen Anne–style mansion in Astoria. He hadn't been to Devlin's home in over a year and had forgotten how its architecture and presence left him in awe. If the outside of the home, with its tan color and gold trim, many bay windows, balconies, and three story tower wasn't impressive enough, then the inside was. With its high ceiling, inlaid hardwood, and beautifully handcrafted woodwork, Devlin had seen to it that every detail displayed only the best craftsmanship available.

When Devlin entered the room Jake smiled and extended his hand. "Good to see you, Devlin," Jake said.

Devlin met Jake's hand and gave him a hearty shake, and then pulled him into a bear hug. "And you, Jake. You're looking well."

"Never felt better," Jake said. "So how have you been?"

"I can't complain." Devlin beelined it for a small table that held a bottle of brandy and glasses on it. Without asking, he poured two glasses. After handing Jake the drink, he motioned for Jake to take a seat on the velvet settee, while he slid into a large overstuffed chair covered in a brocade of gold and accented with gold tassels.

After both men rested Jake said, "I received your telegram."

Devlin's smile quickly faded. "Yes. Unfortunately we have to meet under less than pleasant circumstances."

Jake frowned.

"I need to hire you for your services," Devlin said.

"You want me to track someone for you," Jake said. Curious, he added, "Tell me more."

Dragging in a deep breath, Devlin released a weary sigh. He removed a cigar from a hand-carved box that sat on a round table next to his chair, and offered it to Jake.

With a short wave Jake declined the offer.

Devlin lit the cigar and took a long drag. Smoke plumed out of his mouth and nose as he spoke. "I had the unfortunate luck of happening upon a murder."

Jake's brows shot up and eyes widened. "Whose?"

Devlin shrugged as if the victim's name was unimportant. "He owned a shabby store in town."

"Why was he murdered?"

Devlin made a face before saying, "Perhaps in the heat of the moment. To me the motive is insignificant."

"You saw the murderer," Jake said.

Devlin nodded.

"Why don't you start at the beginning?"

"It was late in the evening and I was taking a leisure-ly stroll, when I heard shouting coming from inside a general mercantile," Devlin said. "When I looked through the store windows I saw a woman stab the owner. As soon as she saw me she ran."

"A woman?" he asked incredulously.

Grim faced, Devlin nodded. "The owner was her uncle." He pushed out of his chair and picked up a pho-tograph that had been laying on the same table as the bottle of brandy. "Here's what she looks like. She's a real beauty." He extended his hand.

Jake took the picture and gazed at it. His chest tight-ened. He couldn't breathe. A knot the size of a boulder formed in his gut. All he could do was stare at Missy's smiling face.

"Her name is Melissa Douglas, but I've been told people call her Missy. She's twenty-two-years-old and traveled to Portland yesterday or possibly the night before," Devlin said.

Feeling Devlin's intent stare on him, Jake collected himself. "She killed her uncle." He had to speak the words out loud, hoping it would seep into his brain.

"I know it's hard to believe." Devlin puffed on his cigar.

Jake glanced back at the photograph. She must have been a few years younger in the picture, but still had that breathtaking smile, glowing eyes, and tempting mouth, a mouth he wanted to savor a hundred times or more. He suppressed the pressure weighing on his heart, along with the immediate desire to defend her, and asked, "So why call me in? Why not go to the marshal?"

"Because I want her found immediately. I won't sleep at night until I know that woman is in jail. She knows I saw her kill her uncle."

"It's hard to imagine a woman so beautiful could do such a horrible thing," Jake said.

Devlin studied him for a moment, the corners of his mouth turned down in a grim expression. His voice filled with anger. "Don't let her pretty face fool you. She's a cold-blooded killer. If she killed her uncle, then she'll have no trouble killing me. You know I'm not only a very wealthy man, but I'm running for the senate. The sooner you find this woman the better."

"Does she have family in the area?" Jake asked.

"Not that I know of. Her uncle wasn't married, nor did he have children. That's why I want you to find her," Devlin said.

Jake frowned. "I don't follow."

"My guess is that she'll head straight for the mountains."

"Wouldn't she try to get to her family?" Jake asked.

"I believe they live back East. And from what I understand, she didn't have much money. In fact it was reported that a woman fitting her description had stowed away on a steamer yesterday. She was chased by two men working on the boat, but they lost her in downtown Portland."

Jake had to inwardly laugh at the seaman's account of what had happened. "Any other information you can think of?" Jake asked. "The more I know about this woman the better chances I'll have of finding her."

Devlin nodded in understanding. "She lived at Sunrise Boardinghouse for Ladies. It's on Jefferson

Street. You might want to talk to the landlady, Mrs. Baker, before you leave."

"What's the marshal doing?"

Devlin snorted. "As far as I know he's giving her time to escape." He rushed on saying, "I tried to get that good-for-nothing marshal out of that position, but to no avail."

"Why would he give her time to escape?" Jake frowned.

"Look at her. He's fooled by her pretty face. He's not thinking with his brain," Devlin said.

"I'll talk to him before I leave tomorrow morning."

Devlin guzzled his drink. "I figured you'd be hungry by the time you arrived, so I had my cook prepare something for us." He motioned for Jake to walk with him. "I feel so much better knowing you'll be helping me."

"You've been a good friend to me, Devlin. I'm glad I finally have the opportunity to return the favor." Jake placed his hand on the man's shoulder and gave him a reassuring smile.

The two men settled at one end of a long table. Devlin provided an elaborate meal of roasted pig, pheasant, sweet potatoes, carrots, hard-boiled eggs, freshly baked bread, creamed butter, honey, jams, and coffee. The conversation turned to business and politics, Devlin's two favorite topics, and to his chances of becoming a senator.

Jake could see the ambition in Devlin's eyes. It reminded Jake of himself eight years ago. Now, that man no longer existed. Jake had lost his passion, that drive and determination to make it to the top. His ambition had cost him his career, dreams, and had cost

Rachael even more—her life. Now he would have to be content letting other men achieve dreams of political office.

As the meal wrapped up Devlin said, "You're more than welcome to stay the night in my home."

"Thank you for the offer, but I've already got a room at the Occident Hotel," Jake said. "I'll be closer to the establishments I need to visit."

"I understand."

"I hate to eat and run, but I've got people to speak with before tomorrow."

Devlin held up his hand. "No need to explain." They pushed themselves out of their chairs and walked to the front door. Shaking Jake's hand, Devlin said, "Send word as soon as you find her. And, uh, if you have an accident at her expense, you'll receive a bonus."

Did he hear him right? Jake said, "Come again."

Devlin grinned. "I think you heard me the first time." He placed his hand on Jake's shoulder, pausing him, "You have two weeks. If you haven't brought her back here by then, I'm putting a bounty on her head." At Jake's surprised expression Devlin added, "I've got too much at stake to have a problem such as this hanging over my head. I'll be traveling around campaigning soon. I don't want to be constantly looking over my shoulder, wondering if she's lurking in the shadows ready to shoot me."

"So she got a good look at you," Jake said, wanting to clarify the details for himself.

"Definitely."

Nodding, Jake said, "I'll do my best."

"I know you will."

Jake gave Devlin a casual salute, and then skipped down the stairs and headed for the boardinghouse. Striding down the steep hill, he gazed out at the harbor. The sun gleamed brightly in a deep blue sky with only a few puffy clouds hanging around. Days like this were rare in Astoria. A cool breeze stirred his hair. Fall had arrived.

With all the Scandinavian immigrants moving into Astoria, the town had its share of boardinghouses. He needed to find the one that Missy had rented from.

Just thinking her name formed a knot in his stomach. Wasn't that his luck? He finally found a woman he fancied and she was wanted for murder. Missy was undoubtedly long gone from Portland by now. He would have to ask around, get a sense for where she might go and what she might do. The way she reacted to him being a tracker now made sense to him. She thought he might have been after her.

He glimpsed at her photograph again. He couldn't imagine her hurting a fly let alone murdering her uncle. He wondered if Devlin was absolutely sure she was the one he saw hovering over the body. He wanted so badly for Devlin to be mistaken.

At the same time, Jake knew looks could be deceiving. Robert Jackson, Rachael's murderer, had been a well-groomed, well-dressed man, who came from a prestigious family in Boston. Yet he turned out to be a murderer of not one but many women.

Even so, he couldn't imagine Missy a murderess. Although, what he thought at this point didn't matter.

He had a job to do for a man he highly respected. He had no choice but to suppress his newfound feelings for Missy and bring her to justice.

Jake found the building and ventured inside. Mrs. Baker turned out to be a tall woman with graying blond hair, tied tightly in a bun at the nape of her neck. Her formal mannerism matched her stiff and erect posture. He smiled at her, yet her mouth remained straight-lined and tight.

Jake extended his hand. "Jacob Gilbert. I'm working on behalf of Mr. McCoy." The mere mention of Devlin's name made the woman's eyes widen. He couldn't tell if he saw fear or respect in them. "I'd like to ask you a few questions about Ms. Douglas and per-haps look in her room."

"Is this about her uncle's murder?" she asked.

"Yes." Jake scanned his surroundings, noting a young woman sitting in the parlor reading a book. "Is there somewhere we could talk more privately?"

Without saying a word, Mrs. Baker pivoted abruptly and strode into a library, the walls were lined with shelves of books on two sides and several chairs were scattered around the room. After Jake stepped inside she shut the double doors.

He waited to gain her attention. "How long had Miss Douglas lived here?"

"About one year."

"Was she a good tenant?"

"Very good. Kept her room neat and tidy. Paid her rent on time." Mrs. Baker's lips squeezed together in a tight white line and her nostrils flared.

"Did she have any gentlemen callers?" Jake couldn't

suppress the knot that sprang to life in his gut as soon as he spit the question out.

Mrs. Baker frowned, eyeing him cautiously. "She was a lady, Mr. Gilbert."

"I didn't mean any offense. I'm only asking because I need to establish whether she had friends or relatives in the area." Jake didn't break eye contact with the woman as he spoke.

Her brows relaxed some as did her lips. "Well, she did have one gentleman caller. He came several times and even took her on a boat ride up the river. He was in the military, a high ranking officer, I believe."

The knot in Jake's gut seemed to enlarge to the size of an apple. "What was the man's name?" he asked, sounding angry, jealous. Dammit, he was.

"I don't remember." When he arched his brows at her she said, "Truly I don't remember. But he was quite a bit older than her, maybe by twenty years."

"Could he have been a relative?"

"Oh, no," she said, emphasizing her answer with a shake of her head. "He was most definitely smitten with her. He even proposed marriage."

Jake's hands fisted at his side. "You're sure of this?"

"She asked me to chaperone her meetings with him. So I was there during his visits. He talked about marriage with her all the time."

"And what was Miss Douglas' reply to this man's proposal?"

Mrs. Baker's light-brown brows drew together. "What exactly are you after Mr. Gilbert?"

Jake instantly realized the error he had made asking his last question, but he hadn't been able to stop himself. He could feel red seeping up his neck and into his cheeks. "As you know she's missing, Mrs. Baker. It's imperative I find her right away. If she accepted this man's marriage proposal, then perhaps I need to find him in order to find Miss Douglas." Okay, he was lying, a lot. And yes, he was more interested in this other man for his own personal reasons. Dammit, he shouldn't care about Missy or her gentleman caller.

"Because you think she murdered her uncle," Mrs. Baker said.

"Because she did murder her uncle," Jake said bluntly.

Mrs. Baker's eyes first widened, and then slitted. Her lips returned to a tight straight line. She folded her arms over her chest.

"Don't you think so?" Jake asked, feeling a bit of hope streak through him.

"Mr. Gilbert. In the year that Miss Douglas was living here I have seen her give what little money she had to children who hadn't eaten in three days; she tended to people who were sick or hurt without asking for anything in return; and I even witnessed her take her shoes off and give them to a woman who had nothing to put on her feet in the middle of winter." Tilting her head to the side, she asked, "Does that sound like a woman who would murder her uncle?"

"How did she get along with her uncle?" Jake asked.

"She thought very highly of him. They went to church together every Sunday. And she helped him at the store everyday."

"She sounds like a saint," Jake said sarcastically. "Have you ever seen her get angry?"

"One time we were walking together from the market and a passing carriage drove through a puddle. The muddy water splashed onto one of her dresses. And you know what she did?"

He shook his head.

"She laughed." Mrs. Baker had a far away gaze in her eyes. "She never did get that stain out."

"We have an eye witness that saw her commit the crime," Jake said.

Mrs. Baker scowled.

Jake could tell she wasn't about to tell him anything more. "Can I see her room now?" Jake needed to remain unattached and clearheaded. If emotions got involved, then he would find it more difficult to track her. But weren't his emotions already involved? He sauntered to the door. Before his hand touched the handle the landlady halted him.

"Mr. Gilbert. It was late and had rained heavily the night Irvine Douglas was murdered. Perhaps Mr. McCoy saw someone who looked like Miss Douglas." She kept a steady stare with Jake until he broke it.

He opened the doors and waited for Mrs. Baker to lead him up the stairs to Missy's room. She opened a door to a small room, which held not much more than a bed, dresser, large trunk, writing desk and chair. "I don't know what you're looking for. All that's in here are her clothes and a few other personal items. And I must say, Mr. Gilbert, I don't feel comfortable allowing you to look through her possessions. If you were working for anyone other than Mr. McCoy, I wouldn't allow it."

"I understand ma'am." He averted his attention to

the room, while Mrs. Baker stood in the doorway watching every move he made like a hawk. Opening the trunk, he shuffled through many dresses, skirts, blouses and underclothing, and then shut the lid. Next, he tried the dresser.

A young girl approached whispering something to Mrs. Baker. "I'm needed in the kitchen," Mrs. Baker said.

"I'll see myself out when I'm finished here," Jake said.

"Very well." Spinning on her heels, Mrs. Baker disappeared around the corner.

On the dresser, Jake found several photographs, a silver comb, and a hand-carved jewelry box. Inside the box was a gold band. Why hadn't she taken the ring with her?

Jake's hand tightened into a fist. He was acting like an idiot, getting jealous over another man interested in Missy. Why was he reacting like this? He couldn't recall the last time he had felt jealous. He just met the woman for goodness sakes! Snapping the lid of the box shut, he focused on the drawers. Shuffling through them, he found nothing.

She hadn't taken much with her. Why? No time, probably? If she hadn't killed her uncle, then why the rush to get out of town?

Closing the drawers, he scanned the room. With nothing left to check, he departed out of the bedroom, exiting the boardinghouse, saying nothing more to Mrs. Baker.

Chapter Five

Jake checked his watch. As he made his way toward the jail, his mind drifted back to Missy's room. He didn't find any signs of bloodstains anywhere, no knife, nothing to indicate she had committed a murder. And true to Mrs. Baker's word, Missy's room had been neat and tidy.

Jake hustled down the street in search of the city jail. As corrupt as Astoria was known to be, the size of the jailhouse didn't reflect it, having only three cells and two desks, one for the marshal and deputy each. He entered the building and approached the desk. "I'm looking for the marshal," Jake said.

"You've found him, son. I'm Marshal Tanner. What can I do for you?"

Jake thought it best not to mention his association with Devlin, since the two were not on good terms with each other. "How do you do, Marshal. My name's Jacob Gilbert."

Marshal Tanner raised his brows. "I've heard of you

and the good work you've done. It's a pleasure to meet you." He extended his hand.

Jake gave the man a firm handshake.

"What can I do for you? Are you working on finding someone?" Marshal Tanner asked.

"Something like that," Jake said. "I'm here to inquire about a murder that happened on the waterfront a few nights ago."

The marshal released a sharp breath. "Which one? Around here we have brawls, shanghais, and murders every week if not every day, especially on Astor Street between Fifth and Tenth."

"This one involved a man named Irvine Douglas."

Marshal Tanner had to be maybe only ten years older than Jake and had straight brown hair, cut short. His hazel eyes never missed anything around him, despite the relaxed manner he projected. Shorter than Jake by at least four inches, the marshal made up for his height with a bulky muscular body.

Tanner frowned. "You're not looking for his niece are you?"

"Actually I am."

"McCoy hire you?"

"Maybe," Jake said, hoping to remain evasive and get information out of him.

"I don't know where the young lady disappeared to. I've searched all over town. All I can say is that I know she's not in Astoria."

"Why haven't you put out wanted posters or notified the authorities in Portland?"

Marshal Tanner narrowed his stare at Jake. "We don't have a telegraph in Astoria. And at the moment I can't afford to send someone to Portland." He continued saying, "Besides, I think it's only fair to give the young lady time to turn herself in."

"Do you have any witnesses besides Mr. McCoy?" Jake asked.

Marshal Tanner released an exaggerated sigh. "Unfortunately it was a stormy night. Not too many people were out and about to see anything. And even if someone did see something out of their window, it would have been difficult to clearly identify the person."

Jake nodded, seeing clearly he would get nothing out of the marshal. "Thank you for your time."

As Jake turned to leave the marshal halted him saying, "If you find Miss Douglas, bring her immediately to me. She'll be safe with me."

"Sounds like you don't think she's guilty," Jake said.

"In the one year that she's lived here, she's probably helped more people in this community than citizens who have lived here their entire lives."

"How so?" Jake asked.

"In church activities like tending to the sick, things like that," Marshal Tanner said.

"What about her relationship with her uncle?"

"They became very close in a short time. She helped him quite a bit."

"In the store," Jake finished for him.

"There too, but I was referring to how she would help him get to and from church—he had only one leg, you know. She made his meals, mended his clothes. She's a gentle women," Marshal Tanner said.

"Sounds like you know her well." Again, Jake couldn't shake the green monster creeping into his gut.

A semigrin formed on the marshal's mouth, but he didn't appear amused. "She worked with my wife at most of the church functions."

Jake was angry at how relieved he felt when he heard Tanner was married. "I see," Jake said, and then quickly changed the subject. "Do you know if she has any family besides her uncle in Oregon or even the Washington Territory?"

"I believe she was engaged to an officer stationed at the Vancouver barracks, but her parents are back East. Her father is Surgeon John Edgar Douglas, a renown surgeon of the Civil War," Tanner said with awe. "I heard he has been nominated for Surgeon General."

"Do you know where her parents are currently living?" Jake asked.

"No." Marshal Tanner shook his head. "I wish I did. I would let them know that their daughter is in serious trouble."

"One more question," Jake said. "I'm wondering when you plan on notifying the authorities in Portland."

Marshal Tanner took his time answering. "Soon."

With a nod Jake said, "Thank you for your time." He departed and headed for his hotel room. Once in the room, he lay down on the bed, propped his hands behind his head and stared up at the ceiling.

"What's going on Missy?" Jake said out loud. Both the marshal and Mrs. Baker didn't think she could have committed this crime, yet Devlin saw her murder her uncle in cold blood. Devlin would have no reason to lie. So she had to have committed the crime. But why?

Devlin said he had heard people shouting. Could

Missy and her uncle have gotten into a heated argument and her uncle attacked her? He released a frustrated sighed. There could be many reasons why she killed her uncle, but what bothered Jake—as it did the marshal—was that he, too, couldn't imagine Missy harming a fly. Of course it wouldn't be up to him to fig-ure out whether she was guilty or not. That would be up to a judge and jury. Once he turned her over to the mar-shal the matter would be out of his hands and Melissa Douglas would be out of his life forever.

Early the next morning, Jake rode the steamer head-ing for Portland. He leaned against the rail and watched the landscape go by at a snail's pace, remaining deep in thought. Suddenly images of a young woman lying in his arms, blood oozing from her throat and staining her green dress flashed through his mind. A shudder raced through his body.

He shook his head in hopes of ridding the memory from his mind permanently, but nothing would ever wash those horrible scenes away. They had been brand-ed into his brain forever. He had ignored the evidence, distorted it to the jury, just to get his client off.

He felt a coldness come over him and harden his heart. Murder was murder was murder. Despite his ini-tial feelings for Missy, he had a job to do. If she was innocent, the truth would eventually come out. If not, then she would get what she deserved. He couldn't let his emotions cloud what was right. Justice had to prevail.

When he returned to Portland he would seek out Missy and bring her back to Astoria. She would pay the price for murdering her uncle. He wouldn't help her go free. Never would he make the same mistake twice, especially when it came to the death of a human being. He wouldn't be fooled by her pretty face and sweet-talk. A credible witness saw her commit the crime. Nothing could excuse what she had done. Nothing.

Missy slapped the last steak in the frypan while Mrs. Baker finished mashing the potatoes. She always loved the smells of supper, sweet and salty mixed together. Checking the butter she had churned yesterday, Missy scooped up a wad and plunked it into a small bowl. Her mind drifted to the telegram she sent a day ago to Surgeon Richard Barnes, a medical doctor at the Vancouver barracks. Why hadn't he answered her plea for help yet? It wasn't like Richard to sit on anything. Perhaps he was still angry with her because she broke off their engagement. She still felt guilty about that, but what was she to do? She had never been in love with the man. Shouldn't that, count for something? Would he refuse to come to Portland to help her even if she said it was urgent?

She couldn't blame him for being upset, but she hoped he could get past that because she needed him now, desperately. What would she do if he didn't come? She knew no one else who would help her.

Out of the corner of her eye she saw the outside door to the kitchen open and Jake step inside.

She flashed him a big smile. She couldn't help it. Just seeing him again gave her joy. Never in her life had she felt like this before. There was just something about this man that attracted her like none other before. "You've returned," she said, turning back to the frypan, pressing the fork on the steak, and listening to it sizzle. "How'd your business trip go?" When he didn't reply she glanced over her shoulder at him.

Jake wore a grim expression. "Miss Douglas, may we speak in private?"

"What's wrong Jake?" Mrs. Baker said, frowning, while whipping a bowl of corn bread batter. "You look like you've just lost your best friend."

He didn't respond.

A dread filled Missy. She wasn't sure how, when, or where, but she knew he had found out. She swallowed. Defiantly, she faced him and said, "Speak your mind. I've done nothing wrong. I have nothing to hide."

"But you do have something to hide, and we both know it," Jake said. "I'm taking you back to Astoria to stand trial for the murder of your uncle."

Mrs. Baker gasped. "Have you lost all your senses, Jacob? This girl here is no murderess."

"I have an eyewitness who says otherwise," Jake said, his stare fastened on Missy.

"He's lying." Missy folded her arms over her chest. "He's the one who murdered my uncle and he's blaming me."

Jake forced a sharp breath out. "You're fooling yourself if you think I'd believe that. Devlin McCoy is one of the most respected men in the state of Oregon. I don't want to hear any more of this nonsense. Come along with me. I'm taking you back."

Tears filled Missy's eyes. Because of his money and power, no one would believe her over McCoy. McCoy had told her that and Jake had just proven his point. "Can I at least get my belongings?"

Jake shrugged. "Sure. But don't take long."

Missy brushed the tears from her face, held her head up high, clenched her teeth, and bristled by him, closing the door to her bedroom.

"Hey," Jake said, "leave the door ajar."

She cracked the door open and poked her head out. "But I have to change into my traveling clothes."

"Well," he said, and then paused as if thinking the matter over, "hurry up."

Missy shut the door once again and placed her bag on the bed. She opened drawers and shut them, making it sound like she was packing and changing her clothes. Padding over to the window, she lifted it open. She glanced at the door, hearing Jake and Mrs. Baker arguing about the situation.

Snatching her small bag of money, in which she had stored the key her uncle had given her, she climbed out the window. Missy searched the area behind the boardinghouse. The place had been recently logged and large stumps covered the ground, looking like ugly worts. To the right of the area, the woods remained untouched and thick. Even though fall had set in, a thick foliage remained year-round in Oregon, making for good hiding places.

At a sprint, Missy headed for the forest's edge. She glanced back only once before disappearing behind a cluster of giant cedars. As she moved farther into the woods, her progress slowed to a crawl. The growth became thick with salmonberry and huckleberry bushes growing everywhere. Underfoot, she contended with bracken fern, wild ginger, fireweed, salal, and Oregon grape, whose stickers jabbed right through her petticoat and stockings.

Somewhere in the distance she heard Jake call her name. Panic surged through her. She had to get away, move faster. She swept aside a branch of a young maple tree and moved deeper into the woods. Between the dark interior and never having been in these woods before, she began to get lost. She stared back at where she had come from, but no longer could tell if that way led back to the beginning or not.

A crow flew overhead, startling Missy. She gasped, but held in the scream. From somewhere behind her she could hear a rustle and knew it had to be Jake coming after her. She held her breath, listening for the sounds to give her a location of where he was. Silence filled the air as if he had also stopped to listen. Then a branch snapped, this time the noise being much closer than before.

Missy's heart pounded in her chest. Her breathing became labored, burning her lungs with each gasp. She stumbled on, thrusting branches out of her way. She heard a ripping sound and knew it came from her dress, but had no time to stop. As she stepped on a small log covered in a thick matting of moss, her foot sank into rotted wood. She tried to catch her fall. Too late. She fell to her knees. Darting a glimpse over her shoulder, she took a gander of the area. There, only maybe fifty yards away, stood Jake.

He appeared not to have seen her. Should she stay hidden or get up and run, giving her hiding place away? Glancing forward, she saw rays of sunlight brightening a patch of a bare and grassy area, a tiny glen in the middle of the forest. A large boulder stood there, looking out of place. A creek ran alongside the boulder. If she could get to the creek, she could follow it. Wouldn't that lead her out of here eventually? Plus, if she treaded through water, she could hide her tracks, which would be smart since Jake was a tracker.

Again, she looked back at Jake. This time, he was crouched down, touching something on the ground. In one swift move, she bounded from her hiding spot. When he called out her name she scrambled faster.

Suddenly she heard heavy footsteps coming after her, the snapping of branches and twigs against her. Sweat trickled down the sides of her face. Her ankles twisted with almost every step she took. By the time she reached the boulder, Jake was only ten yards behind her. Spotting a thick stick on the ground, she picked it up. Whirling around, she clubbed the stick at him. It whizzed by his head, missing him by only an inch.

Startled by the onslaught, Jake darted out of reach. Missy ran toward the creek. She held tight to the stick in her hand, knowing this was her only defense.

Powerful arms grabbed her from behind, wrapping themselves around her, pinning her elbows to her side. He tried to seize the stick, yet she clung tightly to it. Using more force, he ripped it from her grip and threw it behind him. "You're coming with me." He grabbed her hand and began to drag her back into the woods.

She struggled to free herself, fighting him with every ounce of strength she had left. "I'm not going back there. I won't get a fair trial. I did not kill my uncle."

He paused and looked at her, doubt written all over his face.

She bit his hand. He released her momentarily but swiftly caught her with his other hand. Missy brought her free hand back and smacked Jake across the face, her hand stinging from the impact.

The expression on Jake's face was deadly. He looked as if he wanted to kill her. If that's what it took, then that's what she would do: fight to the death. What did she have to lose?

But Jake never gave her the chance. In one swift move, he grabbed both her wrists and pinned her arms behind her back. Her body pressed against his. She could feel his heart pounding from exertion, just like hers. "My God, you're a wild cat."

"You leave me no choice," she said, panting.

"Just like you left your uncle no choice, right Missy?"

She struggled to free herself, but knew instantly it was hopeless. Her body rubbed against his. Looking into his eyes, she saw them changed from anger into something else. His voice came out husky, yet soothing. "Settle down."

Taking several deep breaths, she calmed herself. Once he loosened his hold she took a step back. A wave of exhaustion settled over her. Her body began to shake uncontrollably. In a surprising move, Jake pulled her into in a tight embrace.

A sob burst out from her. She buried her face in his chest. In a muffled voice she said, "I didn't do it. I loved my uncle. I didn't kill him. I swear."

One of Jake's hands came to rest on the back of her head. He said nothing, just continued to hold her.

Lifting her head, she gazed into his eyes. "Why won't you believe me?"

"It doesn't matter if I believe you or not, Missy. I've been hired to bring you back to Astoria to stand trial."

"Hired? By who?" she asked.

"Devlin McCoy."

Just his name ignited the fight in her and she struggled against his grip. Jake's hand tightened on one of her upper arms. When she knew she couldn't free herself she said, "That man is evil. He stabbed my uncle in the chest with his ivory-handled knife. And then—" her voice cracked. She froze, feeling too tired to fight any longer. She wiped her tear-streaked face and runny nose with her sleeve. In a whisper she finished saying, "—he just wiped the blood off of the knife and onto my uncle's pants like he was a wild bore he'd just slaughtered for a feast." A sob caught in her throat. She rubbed her forehead, wishing the memory of what she had seen would go away. Unfortunately at the present time, that's all she could remember. Vaguely she recalled a conversation between the two men, but the details seemed blocked from her memory.

In a voice of despair she said, "He left the store and I ran over to my uncle. He told me to get out of town, that I was in danger. And then he—"

Her head fell forward, back into his chest. Sobs racked her body. She lifted her head and gazed into his confused face. "Why?" she whispered. "Why would he do such a thing to my uncle? We had nothing of value.

If McCoy wanted the store, why didn't he just buy it? He could have paid for it ten times over."

Jake just shook his head. "Come on, let's go."

Missy held her ground, not budging. "Haven't you heard anything I've said?" she demanded. "If I go back to Astoria, McCoy will have me killed. Don't you care?"

"The law will see to it you have a fair trial," Jake said.

She spat a breath out. "Fair trial. Right." Her eyes narrowed to slits. "You honestly believe I'll get a fair trial? Who'll believe me over McCoy? You don't? Why would anyone else?"

"There are lawyers—"

"Lawyers won't do anything. McCoy owns all of them."

"Hire one from Portland, one he doesn't know," Jake said.

"I have no money," Missy said.

"What about your parents? Can't they help you?"

Missy shook her head.

Jake looked around as if he didn't know what else to say or do.

She frowned. "I can't believe you're the same man I met yesterday," she whispered. "You were so kind and caring. Now you're cold and distant."

He didn't respond to her, nor would he look at her. Keeping a firm grip on her, Jake jerked Missy forward. Too tired to resist, Missy followed. Breaking from the forest, the bright sunlight stung her eyes. "It's too late to catch a steamer back to Astoria tonight. We'll stay at the Palace Hotel until morning."

Feeling hopeless, Missy trudged back to Mrs. O'Sullivan's boardinghouse and gathered up her things. Mrs. O'Sullivan gave her a hug before she left with Jake out the back door and into a waiting carriage. Missy felt suddenly like collapsing. With a sigh, she resigned herself to return to Astoria to die.

Chapter Six

Discretely, Jake locked Missy in a room at the Palace Hotel, but gave her the freedom to remain untied. He saw no need to bind and gag her since she couldn't escape from the hotel. And he put her in a room on the second floor just to make sure she couldn't slip out another window. He delivered her meals to her, and left abruptly. No sense in sticking around and listening to her claim her innocence.

Jake had thought long and hard about Missy's declarations. But he kept returning to the same problem: why would Devlin McCoy lie about what he saw? He had seemed so certain of who and what he had seen. Plus, with her uncle owning the store, that did give her a possible motive for theft, even if Irvine Douglas didn't own much.

Jake didn't know what to think. Perhaps it would be best if he didn't think about it at all. But that was difficult to do with the most gorgeous creature to come into his life in a long time—and his attraction to her was undeniable—he could think of nothing else.

Every time he closed his eyes, visions of Missy came to mind. He admired her fighting instinct, even if it had made his job harder. But why should he believe her wild story about Devlin murdering her uncle? Hadn't she lied to him from the moment she met him? He was sure she had lied about being a stowaway, so she could very well be lying now about her uncle. Yet, what bothered him were the comments made by her landlady, Mrs. O'Sullivan, and Marshal Tanner. They seemed to think that it was impossible that Missy could have committed murder.

Jake sighed in frustration. She had the face of an angel. Could she have killed her uncle? She had fought hard against him, even using a stick to try and club him in the head. He stared at his hand, her teeth marks having bruised his skin.

A light knock on the door brought him out of his thoughts. He opened the door to find Simon standing there with a tray. Simon had been the only one Jake had told about Missy and his mission to bring her back to Astoria.

"Here's her dinner," Simon said. After he handed the tray to Jake he pushed his glasses higher on his thin nose. He wore a grim expression.

When Jake met the man's gaze he could tell Simon did not agree with what Jake was doing. What did he care of what Simon thought? He had a job to do and he was doing it. "I'll take it to her."

With a sharp nod, Simon departed.

Jake ambled down a long hall, turning a corner twice

before he came to Missy's room. He had purposely put her away from patrons in the hotel so as to avoid attracting attention. He preferred to conduct business in a subtle way and this situation definitely called for discretion.

He knocked lightly on the door before retrieving the key from his pocket to unlock it. Using his shoulder, he pushed the door wide.

Missy faced the window, her back to him, and arms crossed over her chest. She made no effort to turn or glance in his direction.

"I brought you something to eat," he said.

She said nothing.

"Is there anything else I can bring you?" he asked, feeling guilt seep into his gut and tie a knot there.

This caused her to pivot and face him. Her arms remained crossed over her chest. "I need to send a message to the Vancouver barracks, to Surgeon Richard Barnes." She padded over to a table in the room, the same one Jake had set her meal on, and snatched up a piece of paper. She stepped closer to him, handing him the paper at arm's length. She not only kept her distance physically, but she remained cold and aloof.

Jake realized he would rather have had her fighting him, than be on the receiving end of this attitude. Fighting meant she still cared, cared about him, cared about proving her innocence. He took the paper and slipped it into his pocket. "I'll have my—I'll hire someone to hand-deliver it immediately."

She whispered, "Thank you." Missy returned to the window and stared out.

Jake wondered what she was thinking and feeling.

Despair. Loneliness. Fear. He wanted to comfort her, but what could he say? *He* was the one bringing her back to Astoria. He couldn't lose track of the fact that a murder had been committed, and Missy was the prime suspect.

"This isn't like Richard to ignore my telegram," she muttered.

"Perhaps he's away." Jake felt a twinge of jealousy creep up again. The mere mention of this doctor, a man once engaged to Missy, irritated him like nothing he had ever felt before. Even with Rachael he had never experienced these kinds of emotions. He wasn't quite sure what to do with them.

Missy just shrugged.

Her movement encouraged him to scan down her length, and then back up. Not only was her face perfect, but so was her body. She was pure woman through and through and stirred a man's desires to the fullest.

She glanced over her shoulder at him. "Was there something else, Mr. Gilbert?"

He could feel heat rush to his face. "Uh—no—not unless you'd like me to do anything else for you."

Giving him a challenging look, she spat out, "How about set me free?"

"You know I can't do that."

"Of course. Because you've already condemned me in your mind. I couldn't possibly be telling you the truth and McCoy couldn't possibly be lying. Isn't that right, Mr. Gilbert?"

"I believe everyone is entitled to a fair trial."

"Fair trial," she said sarcastically. "What do you

know of fair trials, especially where Devlin McCoy is concerned?"

"That's the beauty of our country—everyone is equal."

She laughed genuinely, but bitterly. "Now who is the naive one here, Mr. Gilbert?"

Annoyed at her formality, he said, "I told you to call me Jake."

"That's when I thought you were my friend." She narrowed her stare on him. "Normally I don't misjudge someone as badly as I did you. I thought you to be an honorable man, but you proved me wrong."

"I am an honorable man. That's why I'm taking you back."

"You are taking me back to a town that Devlin McCoy controls, the very man who's accusing me of murdering my uncle. And that's what you call justice. I won't get a fair trial. Far from it. That is if I even stay alive until my trial." As if dismissing him, she turned away and remained silent.

Deciding to leave her to her mood, Jake slipped out the door and headed downstairs to hire a messenger to deliver her note to the Vancouver Barracks.

Listening to the key rattle in the lock, Missy glared at the closed door. She could tell Jake desired her. He had the same look in his eyes Richard had had on many occasions. And she had seen women use their wiles on men to get them to do their bidding. The thought had crossed her mind, but she doubted Jake would fall for something like that. He would probably use her and still drag her back to Astoria.

She sunk on the edge of the bed and stared at the window. She rubbed her arms, feeling goose bumps rise on her flesh, despite the warm temperature of the room. Crossing to the window, she pushed the curtain aside and cracked the window open to allow some fresh air into the room.

She noticed a ledge right below her window. Poking her head out, she glanced down at the alley. Wooden boxes were stacked up against the outside of the hotel wall. Her despair started to turn into hope. She would have to plan her escape for late at night or the early morning hours when no one was around. But where would she go?

She had only one choice: the Vancouver barracks. She would go to the barracks and beg Richard to help her. He had never been able to deny her requests before. When he saw her in such distress, she was sure he would come to her aid.

She felt so hopeful she wanted to cry. She had one problem, though—Jake. He was no fool. Would he have a guard outside watching for her escape? He hadn't placed one outside her door.

When he came for her tray she would pretend to be asleep. Hopefully, he would relax enough to let his guard down. Then she would sneak out the window, borrow Mrs. O'Sullivan's horse, and cross the Columbia River over to the Vancouver barracks.

For the first time today she felt hungry. Picking up the plate of food, she gobbled her dinner down.

Jake knocked lightly on her door. When no response came he said, "Missy? May I come in?" Again, no reply. Alarmed, he quickly unlocked the door and stepped inside, shutting the door behind him. The room was dark. He couldn't tell if Missy was there or not. He marched over to the table, lit the lantern and turned it up, illuminating the entire room.

A sleepy Missy sat up in bed, rubbing her eyes. "What's going on?"

Jake could only stare at the vision she made. She was dressed in her chemise, which at the moment had several buttons unfastened and showed her cleavage. Her long black hair had been brushed out and was draped over her shoulders, and her lips, full and pink, were parted in an suggestive way. He found himself holding his breath. He released air from his lungs. "I'm sorry. I didn't mean to wake you. I thought—" Since he could hear the disturbance in his voice, he was sure she could too.

This woman did something to him. She ignited a fire in him he had never known before. He wanted her, and at the moment he felt he would do anything just to have her. "I thought you left."

"How would I do that?" Her voice purred heavy with sleep, a sultry and inviting sound. When he didn't answer she said, "I'm tired. Would you mind leaving? I've got a very long day ahead of me tomorrow."

"Of course." He moved toward the door, but on his way paused beside her bed. Unable to resist, he reached out and placed his hand on the side of her face. "I wish things could have been different for us. Maybe under different circumstances—" She pulled away from his touch and glanced away.

Frustrated and angry, Jake crossed back to the table

and snuffed the lantern out. He hastened out of the room and never looked back. If he had seen her one more time, looking like a goddess in her white chemise, he wouldn't have been able to stop himself from kissing her. He returned to his room and pulled out a full bottle of whiskey. Would this be enough liquor to drown his desires? Would this be enough liquor to bury his guilt? He poured himself a generous glass and downed it in seconds. Then he poured another one.

He had dreamed about a woman like Missy many times over during the last eight years. Now he had her in his life and what was he doing—taking her back to Astoria to be hanged. God. For the second time in his life, he had fallen in love, and the woman would die before his eyes, again, all because of him.

Jake threw the glass across the room, shattering it against the wall. Grabbing the bottle, he focused on nothing but drowning his pain one more time.

Missy waited for Jake's footsteps to disappear on the other side of the door before she flung the covers back. She padded over to the lantern and lit it, keeping the flame low. Having laid her clothes out on a chair, she quickly changed into them. Once she fastened her shoes, she crept over to the window and opened it wide.

She peered out and looked down. With the street lanterns giving off a dull light, she could make out the shapes of the wooden boxes below. Tossing her bag out the window, she heard it land. Missy scanned the area, not seeing anyone in sight. This far back in the alley, she doubted anyone would see or hear her, even if she made a loud noise.

Crawling out on the ledge, she rolled over onto her stomach and lowered herself down. She felt for the window trim of the first floor window just below hers. The toe of her boot touched first. She glanced down and saw the boxes looming like dark shadows. She would have to jump down about a foot to the boxes. Gathering the courage, she let go of her grip.

Both her feet hit the top box at the same time, her right foot crashing right through. A piece of the broken wood cut through her pantaloons and gouged her leg. She sucked in a sharp breath as the pain seared through her.

Tottering on the box, she carefully pulled her leg out. Getting off the boxes proved to be much easier than jumping onto them. She climbed off on her hands and knees, picked up her bag, and dashed out of the alleyway. At the corner, she searched the area. A few gentlemen stood at the front of the hotel, and several hacks were still parked out front. Heading in the opposite direction of the hotel, Missy scampered up the road, keeping to the shadows. She ran several blocks before she headed toward the outskirts of town in the direction of Mrs. O'Sullivan's boardinghouse.

By the time Missy reached Mrs. O'Sullivan's it was late. She entered through the back of the house and found Mrs. O'Sullivan in the kitchen, sitting at the table drinking a brandy. Her eyes widened, seeing Missy. "What in holy name are you doing here?"

"I need your help," Missy said. She quickly told the

older woman her entire story, from going into her uncle's store just before his murder to escaping out the second floor window of the Palace Hotel. "Please help me. I have to get to the Vancouver barracks. My father's good friend, Richard Barnes, is a surgeon who works there. He can help me."

"What do you want me to do?" Mrs. O'Sullivan asked.

"I need to borrow a horse to get to the barracks," Missy said.

Mrs. O'Sullivan contemplated for a moment. Then she said, "You really think this McCoy man will kill you if you return to Astoria?"

"Yes," she said without hesitation. "I need money and power on my side to counter McCoy. Surgeon Richard Barnes can help."

Mrs. O'Sullivan nodded. "Okay then. I'll do you one better. I'll go with you to the river. I have a friend who can get you across tonight."

Relief rushed through every inch of Missy's body. With a choked voice she said, "Thank you."

"Let's get a move on it," Mrs. O'Sullivan said. "Jake will find out you're gone soon enough."

Missy arrived at the barracks late in the evening. A few guards were on duty, but most of the barracks' personnel had gone to sleep. Nevertheless, she knew where Richard would be. She rode straight to the hospital and dismounted. Entering the building, she found a young man working at a desk. He glanced up, surprised to see her. "May I help you?"

"I'm here to see Surgeon Richard Barnes," Missy said.

"He's not here ma'am."

"Is he at his residence?" she asked.

"No ma'am. He should be returning from the Walla Walla post any day now. Would you like to leave him a message?" the young man asked.

"Yes. If I could." The man handed her paper and a pen. She scribbled a note for Richard to meet her at an abandon post about twenty miles east on the Oregon side of the Columbia River. Richard had pointed it out to her when they had taken a boat trip up the river. No one would ever think she would head there. She should be safe there until Richard arrived. Folding the paper in quarters, she handed it back to the young man. "Please. See to it that Surgeon Barnes gets this immediately. It's urgent."

"Yes ma'am."

Missy returned to her horse, but before she could mount a woman spoke to her from behind. In a low threatening voice, she said, "How dare you show your face here?"

Missy turned to find Felda Lawton glaring at her. Felda had never taken the news very well of Richard becoming engaged to Missy, and never treated Missy kindly when she had visited Richard at the fort. A widow in her forties who seemed to never smile, Felda had been Richard's nurse for the last ten years. Her devotion, Missy had always suspected, had been more out of deep feelings for Richard rather than a sense of duty to the Army. Apparently, Felda was proving Missy right.

"Excuse me?" Missy said.

"Don't act like you don't know what I'm talking

about," Felda said through clenched teeth. "You stomped on his feelings when you broke off your engagement to him, and now you're back again, hoping he will give you the time of day. You make me sick."

The woman's venom almost knocked Missy over. She knew the woman never liked her, but her behavior now was shocking. "I'm sorry I hurt Richard. That was never my intent."

"He's too good for the likes of you. He was only marrying you because he felt indebted to your father," Felda said.

"If that were true, then how could I have hurt him?" Missy said, getting a little tired of this woman's insults.

Felda tipped her head back, her eyes narrowing, her plain face contorting in anger, and her nostrils flaring. "Do us all a favor and get on your horse and disappear forever."

"Why? So then you can have Richard all to yourself?"

Felda gasped.

"You don't fool me or anyone else around here. And above all, you don't fool Richard. You're in love with him, yet he doesn't notice you, so you're blaming me for that," Missy said.

Felda swung at Missy, but missed. "I'll make sure Richard never sees you again."

"And you'll have to live with the knowledge that he would much rather see me everyday, than you," Missy said. She climbed her horse and rode out. The minute she reached the river and had time to calm down, she regretted the words she had spoken to Felda. She couldn't afford to have another enemy right now. More importantly, she needed Richard's help. Missy was only slightly comforted with the knowledge that the private in the hospital had her note to Richard and Felda didn't know about it.

She rubbed her face. What else could go wrong in her life? Sticking to her plan, she kept on course, crossed the river, and headed for the abandoned fort. She had nowhere else to go.

Chapter Seven

"Jake. You wanted me to wake you so you could make the early steamer," Simon said, his face inches from Jake's.

Jake groaned. "Go away."

Simon picked up the bottle that lay on the floor and set it on the nightstand. "That whiskey's going to stain the rug. And it smells like a still in here. I won't be able to rent this room out for a month."

"That's good," Jake said, pushing himself to a sitting position. "Because that's how long it'll take me to get over this damn headache."

Simon picked up the bottle again and shook the near empty liquid inside. "Something weighing on your mind, Boss? Or do I need to ask?"

"I'm just doing my job," Jake muttered.

"I've never seen you this interested in a woman before," Simon said. "It was good to see you smile."

Jake sighed. Nothing good ever lasted long with him. He met his friend's concerned look. "I'll live."

"How does a hot pot of coffee sound?" Simon asked.

"Like heaven." Slowly, Jake stood. His head felt like it was about to explode. After Simon exited, Jake ambled over to a basin of water and splashed his face. Nothing seemed to wake him up. He dried himself, and then headed out the door and down the hall. Taking the stairs, he descended to the second floor and meandered through the maze of hallways to the back of the hotel. No one had been put in a room near Missy. He had not wanted anyone to see him going in and out of her room and damage her reputation.

He knocked on the door. "Missy. It's time to get up." No reply. "Missy. Wake up." Still no response. Something wasn't right. Jake placed his key in the door and opened it. His gaze zeroed in on the empty bed, and then to the fluttering curtains. Charging over to the window, he peered out. He spotted the stacks of wooden boxes, the top one with a hole in it. No doubt that was where her foot had fallen through.

"Damn," he mumbled under his breath. Jake whirled around and dashed from the room, but as he passed the door, he slowed down and grabbed his head. By the time he reached his room, he met Simon at the door.

"What's going on?" Simon asked.

"She flew the coup," Jake said. He didn't miss Simon's grin.

"I think you've met your match," Simon said.

Jake changed into his jeans, flannel shirt, and upper

mucking boots. He grabbed his rifleman's coat, but didn't put it on.

"Anything I can do?" Simon asked.

"Yes. If she comes back here, make sure she doesn't leave. Lock her in her room if you have to. And whatever you do don't help her get away. If I don't have her back in Astoria soon, McCoy's going to put a bounty on her head," Jake said.

Simon's eyes widened. "Don't you find that strange?"

Jake ignored the question. It was something Jake had thought too. But then again, he had seen McCoy overreact once or twice before. Jake hastened out the door and out of the hotel. Stopping first at the livery, he saddled and bridled his horse. Straddling his paint, he galloped toward the boardinghouse.

He bolted into the kitchen, spotting Mrs. O'Sullivan cooking at the stove. "Where is she?"

Mrs. O'Sullivan slowly pivoted to face him. "Where is who, dear?"

"You know damn well who I'm talking about," Jake said. "Missy. Where is she?" When she didn't answer he said, "Fine. I'll check every room myself."

Alarmed, Mrs. O'Sullivan halted him saying, "She's not here."

Jake grinned, but he felt far from humored. "So you do know where she is?"

Mrs. O'Sullivan began to wring her hands. "She's all alone, Jake. Someone had to help her. Why can't you be the one to do it? I know you fancy her. I can see it in your eyes, the way you look at her. You're smitten."

"It doesn't matter how I feel about her. She's wanted for murder," he said.

"She didn't do it," Mrs. O'Sullivan stated with confidence.

"And how would you know that?"

"Come on, Jake. Does she act like a murderess? Use your common sense," she said.

"Then the jury will acquit her," he argued.

"She has no lawyer."

He shook his head and his index finger at her. "Oh, no. Don't even suggest it."

Mrs. O'Sullivan pushed ahead as if he hadn't said a word. "At one time you were one of the best lawyers in the country. If anyone could help this lass, you could."

"I haven't practiced in eight years," he said.

"It's like riding a horse. Once you've done it you don't forget how to do it," she said.

"And how would you know this?" he said more as a statement than a question.

Her voice took on a stern motherly tone. "You're like a son to me, Jake. I've known you since you were a baby. And I'm telling you, this girl is special. The two of you have eyes for each other. If you don't help her, you'll be losing the best thing to come into your life."

"Did she say she has eyes for me?" he couldn't resist asking.

Mrs. O'Sullivan smiled. "So you care?"

"I'm just curious, that's all."

She laughed. "You don't fool me, Jacob Gilbert. I've never seen you so smitten with a girl before. Not even Rachael."

"Sometimes I think I made a mistake bringing you out here to run this boardinghouse."

"It's good for you to have someone who knows your past," she said. "Otherwise who would you talk to?"

"You're getting off the subject," he said. "Where's Missy?"

"I'll tell you on one condition." She raised a brow.

"What is it?"

"That you help her. That you act as her lawyer and get to the bottom of this terrible accusation," Mrs. O'Sullivan said.

"Do you have any idea what you're asking me to do?" he questioned.

"Move on from your past," she answered. "You've got to do it sometime. Why not now?"

He met her stare. So many emotions churned inside him. Fear. Guilt. Hope. Despair.

Mrs. O'Sullivan continued and Jake just let her speak her mind. He knew she would tell him where Missy was in her own time. So he waited.

"I know why you were attracted to Missy. She looks very much like Rachael." He glanced away, but she kept talking. "But I knew Rachael, and Missy is nothing like her. Rachael was spoiled and thought only of herself. She wanted the best of everything, and that included you, Jake. You were the best lawyer, the up and coming politician."

"She loved me," Jake argued.

"Perhaps in her own way. But Rachael loved herself most of all. Missy is completely different. That girl has substance. She's a hard worker, and she will stick by you when times get hard."

"How do you know all of this? You've only known her one day," Jake said.

"Because when you get to be my age, Jacob, you learn to read people. I can spot a fake from a block away. And most of those women you've associated with in the past have been all wrong for you. This one isn't." She folded her arms as if ending her statement with an exclamation point.

He sighed, tired of the lecture. "Are you going to tell me where she is or not?"

After a long pause, Mrs. O'Sullivan said, "At the Vancouver barracks."

"Damn," Jake muttered.

"What's wrong?"

"She went to see Surgeon Richard Barnes," he said, feeling that darn jealousy creep into his gut again. Why couldn't he get rid of that feeling? He wasn't used to feeling this emotion at all.

"Yes. I believe that's who she said she needed to see. She said he was her father's acquaintance. What's wrong with that?" Mrs. O'Sullivan's eyes narrowed.

"Because. She was betrothed to the good doctor not too long ago," Jake said. "This will force her back into his arms."

"Not if you get to her first," Mrs. O'Sullivan pointed out, "and convince her you're the better man."

A determination came over Jake, one like he had never known before. No one, not a doctor, not a jury, would take Missy from him. He would get to the bottom of this murder charge even if it meant returning to practicing law. There were some things a man had to fight for in life, and this was one of them.

He kissed Mrs. O'Sullivan on the cheek. "I think I'll keep you."

"Go get her, Jacob. And hurry!"

Jake arrived at the barracks before the afternoon sun. He rode directly to the hospital. When he stepped into the building the young man who greeted him acted as if he knew Jake. The kid looked familiar, but for the life of him, Jake couldn't recall where he had seen him before.

"You don't remember me, do you Mr. Gilbert?"

"I'm sorry, I can't recall," Jake said.

"Private Tom Pickering. You helped me out a few months back, when I was in Portland and got beat up by two men near your hotel. You took me in, had a doctor look me over, gave me a bed for the night, and fed me."

Jake nodded in recognition. "Now I remember. How're you doing?"

"Much better, thank you." Tom smiled. "So what can I do for you, Mr. Gilbert?"

"I'm looking for a young woman by the name of Melissa Douglas. I'm told she came here to find Dr. Richard Barnes," Jake said.

"Yes. She was here. But Surgeon Barnes is away and won't be back for several days. I told Miss Douglas this," Tom said.

"Do you know where she went?" When Tom hesitated Jake said, "It's very important I find her."

Tom sighed. "I shouldn't do this," he said, "but I do owe you one." He searched the desk, but couldn't find what he was looking for. "It was here last night, but now it's gone."

"What?" Jake asked.

A woman bustled into the room and busied herself at one of the desks.

"Mrs. Lawton," Tom said. "Do you know what happened to a piece of paper that was on my desk? It was addressed to Surgeon Barnes."

She hesitated a glance in the private's direction, but couldn't meet his eyes. "I'm not sure." She turned back to her desk.

Jake watched the woman. She had done something with the note, no doubt about it. Guilt was written all over her face. He didn't need to be a genius to figure out why. The older woman, for some reason, didn't want Missy back in Surgeon Barnes' life. Well, that was fine with Jake. He didn't want the good old doctor in her life either. But he still needed to know where she went. He returned his attention back to the private.

Tom scribbled something on a piece of paper. In a low voice he said, "Don't tell anyone I gave you this." He glanced over at Mrs. Lawton, but she acted as if she hadn't heard a word he'd said.

Jake took the paper and read it. He handed it back to Tom. "Looks like we're even. Much obliged Tom," He nodded, and headed for the door. Pausing, he pivoted. "Next time you're in the neighborhood, come visit me. You'll always have a place to stay." With a salute he exited the building, and then sauntered over to his horse and mounted. He checked the position of the sun. By this evening he should have caught up with Missy. And when he catches her this time, he'll make sure she doesn't get away again.

* * *

By the time Jake arrived at the abandoned post the sun had set and a full moon appeared in the flawless night sky. Over the years, he had learned to adjust to the dark and didn't have much of a problem seeing in very little light. He found Missy had unsaddled and unbridled her horse and placed it in the abandoned stables, one of the buildings in pretty good shape. After he settled his horse in for the night, he slung the saddlebag and canteen over his shoulder. With his rifle in hand he walked to the closest building, an old guard house.

Jake pushed the door wide and stepped inside. The moon lit the room just enough to see a silhouette rushing toward him. Missy. He knew she couldn't see his face. In a surprised move, she flung her arms around him.

"Oh, Richard. I knew you'd come. I knew I could depend on you. Please help me." Her voice choked, before sobs spewed forth. Her body shook like a leaf fluttering in the wind.

Jake wasn't sure what to do, so he just stroked her hair and whispered, "It'll be all right."

She clung to him with her head on his shoulder. Like she hadn't heard him speak, she said, "I didn't do it. I swear. I'm so scared. I've got a man chasing me. And Devlin McCoy is lying." She gulped a breath. "Richard. If you help me, I'll do anything. I'll marry you if that's what you want."

Jake's hand froze, and then dropped to his side. Did she just agree to marry him out of desperation, or did she love the man? His hand curled into a fist as jealousy rose in his gut. Impulsively and in an angry voice he said, "So if I help you, Missy, will you marry me?"

Missy's body stiffened. She jerked out of his hold and took several steps away. "Jake. How'd you find me?"

He kicked the door shut with the heel of his foot. He saw her head jerked toward the door. "Don't even think of escaping this time." A coyote howled in the distance. "You hear that? Those wild animals hunt at night. They'll eat you alive." He pulled out a few candles and lit them, thumping them on a crudely made table that stood in the middle of the room.

Shadows still hid half of her face, but he could see the tears that streaked her cheeks. She stood erect, her arms crossed over her chest, and her eyes watching his every move.

"You want something to eat?"

She licked her lips and gazed hungrily at the dried meat and bread he pulled out. She made no move to accept his gifts.

"I bet you thought you'd be eating in the officer's fancy dining room right about now, didn't you?"

"What do you mean?" Missy said in a challenging tone.

Jake shrugged. "You figured you would have found the good old doctor at the barracks and you'd be safe and sound in his arms once again." He couldn't keep the edge out of his voice, nor did he try. He wanted desperately to punch the doc in the nose, and he had never even met the man.

"At least I could count on him to help me. He wouldn't be so quick to rush me back to Astoria, just to see me hang for a crime I didn't commit," she said.

"That's where you're wrong, Missy," Jake said.

"My name is Miss Douglas to you."

Jake grinned, despite the anger still boiling inside him. "Sit down, Miss Douglas." When she didn't move he barked out, "Sit down." He yanked out a chair and waited for her to plant her pretty bottom in it. He placed his hands on the back of her chair and leaned down, placing his mouth next to her ear. "That's where you're wrong. Your precious Richard would have you back in Astoria faster than you could blink your eyes."

Her head jerked in his direction, their lips only an inch apart. Her eyes dipped to his mouth before she looked away.

Fire erupted inside Jake like an explosion of dynamite. Needing a distraction, he treaded away, and plunked down in a chair, keeping the table between them. He studied her. Despite her disheveled appearance, her red swollen eyes, and pouting mouth, she had never looked more beautiful to him than she did at this moment.

He pulled out an apple and a knife and began to cut slices off. He crunched the succulent red fruit, wondering if Missy's lips would taste even sweeter. "You'd better eat up. We've got a long day ahead of us tomorrow."

"Not if Richard arrives before we leave," Missy said.

God, he wished she would stop mentioning that man's name. "I hate to disappoint you, but Richard isn't coming."

"But the private said—"

"I'm all you've got. I'm the only one who can get you out of this mess," he said, liking the fact that he could help her more than Richard could.

She expelled a sharp breath. "How could you help me? And why would you?"

"How? Because I'm a lawyer. I used to be a very good one in criminal law. And why?" He paused long enough for effect, just as he had done many times in the courtroom. "Because you're going to marry me once I get you off."

She jolted out of her chair, the legs screeching on the hardwood floor. "Why would I marry a man I don't love?"

Her comment jabbed him in the gut. He kept his ire in check. "You just offered to marry Surgeon Richard Barnes and you don't love him."

She paced several feet away, keeping her back to him. "How do you know I don't love him?"

He grinned. He could hear her answer in her voice. "Why else would you have broken your engagement off with him?"

She whirled around, her eyes wide. "How did you find out about that?"

"Oh," he said lightly. "Did I strike a nerve?"

"You are the most infuriating man I've ever met," she said. She suddenly charged for the door, but didn't make it past Jake.

Dropping the knife, he grabbed her around the waist and pulled her onto his lap. "So do we have a deal, darling?" She pushed on his chest to escape his clutches. In an attempt to taunt her further, he kissed her. He hadn't expected the kiss to effect both of them, but it did. Missy stopped fighting, her body slowly relaxing into him. Deepening the kiss, Jake slid his hand up her back and came to rest on the nape of her neck. When they broke the kiss they gazed into each others' eyes.

Jake vaulted out of the chair, setting Missy aside. He paced to the other side of the room, running his fingers through his hair. Taking deep breaths, he regained his composure. She bewitched him. How could any woman have this much power over him? He strode outside and sat down on the front step. Pulling out a cigarette, he lit it and smoked it slowly. He didn't smoke very often, but damn he needed a smoke right now.

Chapter Eight

He took a long drag, wishing he had a glass of whiskey to go along with his cigarette. If he were to help Missy out, he would have to get her to open up to him, tell him everything she knew about her uncle's murder, Devlin's involvement, and the conditions of the night. So many things about this murder didn't add up, and hadn't from the start.

Why would Devlin encourage him to kill Missy instead of have her stand trial if she really had killed her uncle? Why put a bounty on her head so quickly? Missy was hardly the type to pose a threat to Devlin, or anyone for that matter. And another thing, why would Devlin have been taking a walk in such bad weather? Both Mrs. Baker and Marshal Tanner claimed the weather had been horrible and visibility almost impossible. Plus, why would Devlin have taken a walk in that part of town? Why not walk in a much safer and upscale area closer to his home?

A sudden frightened whinny came from the barn. Soon, both horses were hysterical. Cougar. He jumped to his feet and dashed inside the building. He reached for his saddlebag and grabbed a handful of shells. "Stay here. Don't go outside unless I call you." Snatching his rifle, he raced outside.

Just as he reached the barn doors, both steeds bolted out. The door whipped open, hitting Jake in the head and knocking him to the ground. His gun flew out of his hands. From inside the barn he heard the wild cat's threatening snarls and hisses. Slowly, deliberately, Jake crawled on his stomach over to his rifle, but before he could wrap his hands around it the cat stood in front of him. The moonlight flashed on his white fangs.

The cat crouched low, waiting to spring. Jake froze. Again, the mountain lion let out a fierce scream as if challenging Jake to make the first move. Just as the cat was ready to pounce, the crack of a gun went off from somewhere behind Jake. He glanced at his rifle only a few feet away from him, confused as to the source of the gunfire.

Another explosion rang. This time the bullet hit the ground only inches from the cat. The mountain lion jumped in fright, and then turned and scampered away. Slowly, Jake sat up.

Missy ran over to him. "Are you all right? Did he attack you?"

"No. I'm fine," he said, confused. He glanced at her hand, her fingers still resting on the trigger. "Where'd you learn to shoot like that?"

"My father's in the military," she said as if the answer was simple. "He made me take target practice.

He said if I knew how to handle a gun it would make me more independent."

Jake rubbed the back of his neck before pushing himself to a standing position. "We'll have to find our mounts in the morning. It's too late and too dark to find them now. Let's just hope we find them before the mountain lion does."

Missy walked beside him into the building. "You're bleeding," she said. "Let me take a look at that."

"I'm fine." Jake could feel the trickle of blood dripping down the side of his face. His pride was more wounded than his head. He had a hard head.

She turned her back to him and lifted her skirt, ripping off a piece of her chemise. Wetting it with the water from his canteen, she dabbed at his head, wiping up the wound, and then applying pressure to stop the bleeding. For a long time they remained silent as she worked on him. Finally she asked, "Did you mean what you said? You could help me?"

"Yes."

"You're really a lawyer?" she asked.

"Yes."

"Why didn't you tell me that when we first met? You told me you were a tracker," she said.

"I haven't practiced law in awhile," he admitted.

Her voice became very quiet, very serious. "Can I trust you, Jake?"

He gazed into her eyes. "Yes."

She licked her lips, and then bit her lower one. "Okay. You've got a deal."

He frowned, unsure of what she was talking about. "I'm confused."

"I'll marry you if you get me off," she said.

Wow. Had *he* been serious when he had said that? He wasn't sure himself. Just the idea of marriage frightened him. But one glance at Missy told him he would get her no other way. And he wanted her like he had wanted no other woman. "It won't be easy."

"Living with you?" she asked. She was teasing him.

"That and getting you off," he said. "You'll have to tell me everything and don't leave out any details."

"When? Now?"

He smiled. "No. For now we sleep. Tomorrow we have to track down the horses. We'll be walking a long way. So we need our rest." He jerked his head toward the saddlebag. "There's a blanket in there. Take it. Those beds don't look too bad. Hard, but in good condition."

"Where will you sleep?" she asked.

He grinned, knowing where he would like to be sleeping. Instead he took the bed next to hers. She might have agreed to his offer, but he still wasn't convinced she trusted him and would not flee given the opportunity. Plus, he wasn't completely sure she meant what she'd said about marrying him. Hadn't she agreed to marry Surgeon Richard Barnes, only to call off the engagement? Jake wondered if she would do the same to him once he got her off?

An hour after they laid down to sleep, Jake remained awake. He could hear Missy shivering, her teeth chattering. The night temperatures had dropped considerably. As a tracker he had learned about the elements, and the sudden changes in the weather, especially on Mt. Hood. He recalled one time he had gotten stuck in a hail storm in the middle of summer. The storm had come up without warning. Life on the mountain could be harsh, and it could be glorious. But a person had to learn to respect the land and expect the unexpected.

He climbed off his hard bedframe and crawled onto hers. Wrapping his arms around her, he cuddled her, hoping his body heat would warm her. Many minutes ticked away before she slowly relaxed. Soon, she began to doze.

Jake lay awake a little while longer, listening to the wind blowing through the trees, the crickets chirping, and the lone coyote howling in the distance. Then he fell into slumber, not waking until morning.

Missy woke to the sound of birds singing outside. The sun shone through the windows, yet she could still see her breath in the air. Jake's arm was draped around her, his body giving her warmth and comfort. She vaguely remembered him coming over in the night to share her bed.

Since she was this close to Jake, she decided to check his head. The gash had looked nasty last night, even in the dim candlelight. She turned his head to the side. The wound didn't look any better in the daylight.

He stirred. A funny grin formed on his mouth. In a sleepy tone he said, "I think I could get used to waking up with you beside me every morning."

She ignored him and said, "I could stitch that gash on your head. Then it wouldn't leave such a big scar."

"I think I'll pass. I'm not one for having someone stick a needle in my skull," he said.

"I'm very quick with my hands," she said.

He stood, stretching his arms over his head.

"Thanks, but no thanks." Opening his saddlebag, he pulled out the bread and dried meat, along with another apple. "Here. We'd better eat something before we move out. I'm not sure how far our mounts ran last night."

"Do you think we can find them?"

He smiled. "Are you forgetting I'm a tracker?"

"You're a lawyer and a tracker?" She sounded confused. "What a combination. How did that come about?"

"When I moved out here I didn't want to practice law any longer. I was in pretty bad shape," he said.

"Were you hurt?" she asked.

"No." He hesitated before saying, "I had lost a loved one. My fiancée. She was murdered and died in my arms."

In a whisper Missy said, "I'm so sorry. I had no idea."

"Well, it's not something I like to talk about. Anyway, when I was looking to invest in businesses in town I met Devlin McCoy. He was selling his cabin and land on Mt. Hood and I looked at it. Then he warned me about a crazy Indian who lived on the mountain. He said the man was called Indian Joe, and that he was harmless, but would steal you blind." Jake shrugged. "I bought the place regardless. All I wanted was to get away from people, and be alone to think."

"And you met Indian Joe on the mountain," she said.

"Yes. But he never stole from me. In fact, he saw what a mess I was in at the time and decided to help me. In return I would give him a place to stay and food to eat any time he came by," Jake said.

"What did you do?" she asked, munching on a slice of apple.

"I agreed."

"So how did he help you?"

Jake raised a brow. "Interested in me, huh?"

Her blushing answered his question. She guessed as a tracker he could read her face as well as he read animal tracks.

He continued. "He taught me the art of tracking. We started with small animals like the racoon and deer mouse and progressed up to elk, cougar, and bear."

"How long have you tracked for?" she asked.

"I've lived here eight years and it took me several years to learn. So about five years. I still have much to learn. Indian Joe had tracked his entire life and he had to have been near eighty when he died," Jake said.

She could hear the sadness in his voice. "How long has he been dead?"

"Two years. That's why I began investing more in businesses in town, so I could have more contact with people. Indian Joe taught me that it was important to get back into society and be around people. I had to admit I missed it," he said.

"I think I understand," she said. "Being a lawyer, you would have been around a lot of people all the time. People coming to you, wanting you to help them. Were you really that good?"

Jake met her eyes. "I was the best. I've never lost a case." He quickly changed the subject. "Come on. Eat up. We've got a lot of area to cover."

Missy had so many other questions she wanted to ask him. She wanted to know about his fiancée. He must have loved her deeply if it tore him up inside so much. She wondered what this other woman looked like. Did she fail in comparison? Would Jake ever come to love her as much as he had loved this other woman?

She knew she shouldn't care so much, but she did. She felt something for Jake and had since the moment she had met him. And when he'd kissed her last night, she felt something she had never felt before in her life. She had wanted more kisses from him, to feel more of the tingling running up and down her spine. Richard's kisses had never made her feel anything remotely like that. The way Jake's touch made her react frightened, yet excited her. She wanted more, but was afraid her resistance to him would dissolve if he gave her more.

"You ready?" he asked, stuffing the food and blanket back into the saddlebag.

She followed him out the door and into the barn, where they picked up the bridles. Jake carried his saddle on his back, but left hers behind.

At first as they headed away from the barn and toward the mountains, Jake just glanced at the ground, following some tracks he obviously saw. She hoped he knew what he was doing, because she didn't see a thing. Once they got into the mountains, Jake occasionally bent down on his hands and knees to study the dirt. He claimed there was a track there, and Missy, after awhile, decided to take his word for it.

"My gelding is heading for my cabin. It'll take us out of the way, slow us down some in getting back to town," Jake said.

Missy was hardly upset by the news. The sooner they

got back to town, the sooner she would return to Astoria and to her hanging. No. She could wait for that.

As the terrain became steeper, Missy had a harder time keeping up with Jake. Despite him carrying a saddle, saddlebag, canteen and rifle, and she only carrying the bridles and her bag, she still had to jog at times to remain close by him. She decided that skirts weren't conducive to climbing all over a mountain.

She didn't complain the entire time, because to do so would go against everything her father had taught her. But she was exhausted, sweaty, and needed a rest. Little by little she lagged farther behind.

Finally, when Jake disappeared from sight, she plopped down on a nearby rock. She would kill for a nap right now. Perhaps that was a bad choice of words, given she was wanted for murder. Jail even sounded better to her rather than traipsing all over the rough mountain landscape.

Appearing out of nowhere, Jake said, "I'm getting close. Stay here. I'll come back for you." He set the saddle and saddlebag down, and picked up a bridle. "And whatever you do, don't go off anywhere. You could get hurt." He took a few steps and then added, "Oh, you might want to have your gun handy, just in case."

Nodding because she was too tired to answer, she opened her bag and pulled out the Colt .45 that Mrs. O'Sullivan had given her for protection, checked to see if it was loaded, and then laid it across her lap. She struggled to stay awake, finally giving in to the need for sleep, sliding to the ground and curling into a ball on a soft matting of moss.

*   *   *

Jake returned with his paint to find Missy asleep. He knew he had been pushing her hard, but he wanted to find his horse quickly. Gazing at the sky, he saw the black clouds moving toward them in the distance. He was hoping to reach his cabin before the clouds unleashed their fury.

Even saddling his horse didn't stir Missy. She looked like an angel, so peaceful and content. "Missy. Wake up."

Opening her eyes, she blinked as if trying to orient herself. "I must have dozed off."

"Come on." He jerked his head toward the horse. "Mount up."

She stood and stared at the horse and saddle. "How am I supposed to ride? There's no ladies' saddle on here."

"You're going to have to straddle the horse," he said.

"But it wouldn't be proper. My legs will show."

Jake lifted her onto the saddle, and then hopped on behind her. He chuckled in her ear. "Do you know how many ladies' bare legs I've seen?"

She gasped. "Well you haven't seen mine," she said tugging her skirt down to hide her exposed ankles."

He drew in a breath. "No, but I'd sure like to." He could see her cheek redden. When she remained silent he said, "I guess I'll just have to wait until we're married. Right?" He tightened his arms around her as he adjusted his grip on the reins.

She glanced over her shoulder at him. "You first have to clear me of my uncle's murder."

"True. But that shouldn't be too hard to do . . . if you're innocent," he said.

"I am," she bit back. She faced forward. "Besides, if

you really thought I was guilty, then why would you want to marry me?"

"Oh, the lady has a winning argument," Jake said. "I guess you caught me there."

Again, she looked at him. But this time her smile just about knocked the wind from his lungs. God she was a beauty. He wondered if he would marry her even if it turned out she had killed her uncle. He was a weak man when it came to this woman. He hoped she never found that out.

They rode for most of the day. Jake knew these woods like the back of his hand and took many short-cuts. By the time they reached his cabin, the sun had been swallowed up by black clouds. He rode over to his barn and dismounted to open the door. Just as his feet hit the ground he heard the rustling of a bush from behind him. At first he thought it was the mare Missy had borrowed from Mrs. O'Sullivan that had followed them back here. Then he spotted it. A long barrel of a rifle sticking out from the corner of the cabin. Jake grabbed Missy, but the gun exploded before they hit the ground. Jake felt the hit instantly in his left shoulder.

He heard Missy gasping for air. Landing hard on top of her, he must have knocked the wind from her lungs. He rolled off and played dead. His gelding danced in a circle before scattering. Jake peeked at his rifle and Colt revolver, still in their sheaths on the saddle as his horse rode off. But he had one last weapon, a spear-point side knife, hidden in a sheath inside his boot. The knife was old and dull, but twelve inches in length. If he aimed right he could at least wound his attacker.

During the commotion, Jake reached for the knife. Then he posed dead on the ground, lying on his side.

Having found her voice, Missy shook him. "Jake. Wake up." He could hear the panic in her voice. She sucked in a sharp breath. Jake heard more than saw the man appear from the side of the cabin. He cocked his gun and chuckled as he neared. Missy grip tightened on Jake's arm.

"I must say," the gunman said. "I've never killed a woman before. Guess it's no different than a man. Still."

A murderer with a conscience, Jake thought. He wanted to shake his head, but remained still instead.

"Who are you?" Missy demanded, her voice choked with emotion. "I have a right to know." She released her grip on Jake to wipe a tear.

"Tom Flynn. And I've been hired to kill the both of you. Can't leave a witness, yah know," he said. "I've got one down. Now all I've got to do is kill you and I'll be on my way."

"Who hired you?" she asked.

"You don't know?"

"Devlin McCoy," Missy said.

From the corner of his eye, Jake saw the gunman lower his rifle, pointing the barrel on the ground. Before Flynn could answer Missy, Jake flipped over and threw his knife directly at the man's heart. A thud could be heard as the knife hit square in the man's chest. The shocked expression on Tom Flynn's face said it all as he fell on his back. Jake sprang to his feet and grabbed for the fallen rifle. He stood over Tom Flynn. Flynn took a final gasp of air, and then expired.

Chapter Nine

With cold anger surging through him Jake dug through the man's pockets, searching for papers or any kind of written agreement. He suspected Devlin McCoy had sent Flynn, but Jake wanted to know for sure. Instead of written instructions, he found wads of money. Who else, besides McCoy, could have paid this handsomely?

He gazed over at Missy. She looked in shock. "Missy," he said. He returned to her side and held her.

Her body shook. "Is he?"

"Yes."

"You killed him?"

"Yes."

She buried her face in his shoulder. "This is so much like what happened to my uncle."

He raised his hand to stroke her hair, but stopped short. Shooting pain raced through his shoulder and down his arm. Glancing at his bloodstained shirt, he felt light-headed. "Missy," he said, "I need your help."

She pulled back. "Oh, my goodness, look at you. Come on. Let's get you into the house." The raindrops began to fall from the sky. With haste, she placed his good arm around her shoulder and helped him into the cabin. The interior of the cabin felt cool. Jake began to shiver. He knew it was more from the shock his body had just received rather than the temperature inside the cabin and damp clothes.

"Sit down," Missy said, guiding Jake over to the bed. "I'll get a fire going, and then tend to your wound. If you feel dizzy, lie back on the bed."

Jake focused on Missy, hoping to keep his mind off the throbbing in his arm and shoulder. He suspected the wound wasn't fatal, otherwise he would be passed out or bleeding profusely, but damn it hurt.

Missy took very little time getting a fire going in the fireplace and in the stove. She filled a kettle full of water and placed it on the stove to heat up. Next, she poured water into a bowl and set it on a table next to his bed. "We need to get your shirt off," she said, "so I can take a look at the wound." She began to unbutton his shirt, carefully removing it on his hurt shoulder.

"There's a lot of blood here," she said. Turning her back to him, she ripped off more of her chemise to use as a cloth and cleaned the wound.

"As much as I enjoy watching you rip a little of your clothing away at a time, I do have linen cloths in that cupboard over there," Jake said, grinning.

Missy's face turned bright red. "You could have told me that a little sooner." She padded over to the cupboard and opened the door. Before she returned, Jake went around the room lighting the lanterns. The sky outside had darkened the room, making it appear to be nighttime.

"Do you have a needle and thread?" she asked.

He joined her at the cupboard and pulled out a pint. Then he opened a drawer and handed her a buckskin pouch, which contained a large needle, Stout linen thread, a paper of pins, beeswax, and thimble.

"I would like a small glass of your whiskey," Missy said.

Jake rose his brows. He shouldn't be surprised. She had been through a lot in the last few days. And now more than ever he believed she had been telling the truth all along. She had been nothing more than a pawn of McCoy's, used as a scapegoat for a murder he committed. There was no other explanation for why Devlin had the hired killer try to kill him as well as Missy. But why? Why would Devlin want him killed? Maybe Devlin didn't want any witness to Missy's murder? Jake could only speculate.

They returned to the bed. Jake sat down, opened the whiskey with his teeth and poured a glass for Missy. He handed her the glass before he chugged down several large gulps of the golden brew right from the bottle. The warmth of the whiskey flowed through him. Suddenly his arm stung like the dickens. "What the heck are you doing?" he asked.

"Pouring the whiskey on your wound," Missy said. "My father said it helps clean it."

"That's a waste of good whiskey," Jake said, frowning.

"Would you rather have infection set in?" she asked.

Jake was amazed at how quickly Missy could stitch an opened wound. The needle and threat went through his flesh so fast he barely had time to feel the prick. As the alcohol took effect, he began to feel tired. He kept drinking as she sewed. Soon the bottle was done. Just as she finished bandaging him up, he lay down on the bed and patted it. Slurring his words he said, "Missy, my love. You'll be forced to share the bed with me. I know it's not proper, before our wedding, but it's all we have. We must make do with what we've got." Jake dozed off.

Missy knew she had much to do before she could go to sleep for the night. She had a body to wrap up and store in the barn, a horse to find and put down for the night, and her sanity to regain. Before she came out West, she had heard it was primitive and hard. Now she knew what that meant. Jake had hardly seemed shaken after he had killed the man. Sure, he hadn't had a choice, but still—he had just taken a human life, just as Devlin McCoy had taken her uncle's life. Shouldn't they feel some remorse or something?

Stepping outside, the rain had turned to mist. Her tears added to the moisture wetting her face. She hadn't had a chance to grieve for her uncle. All her pent up emotions spewed forth as she yanked the knife from Flynn's chest and wrapped his wet body in a sheet, dragging him into the barn. She set his body on top of a bed of straw, and then ran outside. She wretched until her stomach had nothing left in it. Falling on her knees, she let the tears flow. Her body shook uncontrollably and she hugged herself. Flashes of Flynn's barrel pointed directly at her as he crossed the yard kept going through her mind. She shook her head to rid herself of them, but nothing worked. She had almost lost her life today, and she thought Jake had died. Now, his life was still in great danger, all because of her.

Her temptation to run away was strong. Then she remembered Jake lying in bed with a gunshot wound to his shoulder. Luckily the bullet had passed through and no main arteries had been hit. He would survive, yet she wouldn't leave him. She couldn't leave him. And not just because he said he could get her acquitted. Her feelings for Jake kept growing deeper each day. Every time he smiled at her or touched her she shivered. No man had ever made her shiver before. When she had kissed him last night the kiss had just about knocked her off her feet. She should have known instantly it wasn't Richard, because of his gentle stroke and broader body. She rubbed her arms, wishing Jake was holding her right now. She needed his comfort and protection. She needed him.

A horse's whinny interrupted her thoughts. At the barn door stood Jake's gelding. Missy wiped her mouth with the back of her hand and stepped slowly over to the pinto. "It's okay," she whispered as she grasped the reins and led the horse inside. As soon as she opened a stall the gelding strolled right in. She removed the saddle and bridle before giving the horse hay and grain. She brushed him down and patted his neck. Wanting only to get back into the cabin, she hurried out of the stall. She avoided glancing at the dead body as she left the barn.

The next morning Jake woke up to the smells of hot coffee, freshly baked biscuits, and cooked ham and eggs. His stomach growled. He rolled out of bed with a groan. His arm throbbed as did his head. Plopping himself into a chair at the table, he watched Missy scurry about the kitchen. "Where'd you sleep last night?" he asked, rubbing his face in an effort to wake up.

"In the chair." She nodded toward the rocking chair he had in the corner of the room, while setting a cup of coffee in front of Jake. "How's your shoulder feeling?"

"Sore."

"You're lucky the bullet went clean through you and didn't hit anything major," she said.

"I'm lucky you were here to help me," Jake said, keeping a steady stare on her.

She didn't smile. "That reminds me. I wrapped the body up and dragged him into the barn. And I stabled your horse."

"Thank you." He hesitated before he said, "Missy. We have to get to Astoria as soon as possible."

She whirled around and frowned at him. "Why?"

"Because McCoy knows where we are. When Flynn doesn't return soon, McCoy will send out another killer. Our best bet for staying alive is to get into Astoria and let the courts process your case," Jake said.

"And while I'm sitting in jail McCoy will pay another assassin to kill me," Missy said.

"No he won't," Jake said with confidence. "I'll put a stop to that."

"How?"

"Just let me handle that," Jake said. He knew if he exposed McCoy's attempted murder plot that any further attempt on Missy's life would lead directly to

McCoy, ruining any chances of the man getting elected into office.

Missy set the meal on the table and sat down across from him. She barely ate anything, mainly picking at her food.

"After we eat we'll head off the mountain. I want to reach the boardinghouse by evening. We'll stay there tonight, get cleaned up, and then head out for Astoria on the six o'clock steamer," Jake said.

She nodded, remaining quiet through the rest of the meal.

Jake helped clean up as best he could with one good arm. "I've got an extra poncho in the barn for you. Looks like rain again today."

"What will we do with the body?" Missy asked.

"I have neighbors at the base of the mountain. I'll ask them to bring the body into Portland with a note to the marshal." Jake headed for the door to saddle and bridle his gelding.

"We should put your arm in a sling," Missy said, halting him at the threshold.

"You can do that before we leave." He stepped into the yard, noticing for the first time how the leaves were turning red, yellow, and orange. He saw the fear in her eyes. He couldn't blame her. She'd almost been killed yesterday. Jake wasn't sure how he could have been so wrong about Devlin. He had never seen this side of McCoy and hoped to never see it again. Fear did funny things to men. For some reason McCoy killed Missy's uncle, Irwin Douglas, but he hadn't planned on an eyewitness to the crime. Instead of being a complication to the murder, Missy became a useful accessory and

McCoy simply accused her of the deed. Like McCoy said, who would believe Missy over him. Even Jake, a lawyer, trained to find holes in people's stories, believed McCoy at face value.

So why would McCoy kill Missy's uncle? He didn't see an obvious reason.

Now that Jake was on McCoy's murderous list he was more determined than ever to bring McCoy down and prove Missy's innocence. Jake wondered if he would hold Missy to her agreement to marry him if he got her off. He wasn't sure. The thought of not having her in his life scared him. But the idea of forcing her to be his wife when he might not be her first choice wasn't that appealing either.

By the time Missy met him in the barn the rain was coming down in steady drops. Jake had already donned his poncho and felt hat.

"Is he still there?" She wouldn't look in Flynn's direction.

"Yes and he's beginning to smell. We'll have to shut the barn up so no wild animals get in," Jake said.

She glanced over at the wagon set in one corner of the barn. "Why aren't we riding in that?"

"Because it would take twice as long to get to town. On horseback we can take shortcuts through the woods. Besides, I want to avoid the main roads." He met her stare, and again, saw fear in her eyes.

Jake placed a poncho over her head and then a straw hat. With his finger under her chin, he gazed into her eyes. "I'll be okay. Everything will turn out fine. Trust me."

She could not even crack a smile. "Let me put your arm in a sling."

He shook her off. "No. I'll be fine." He kissed her lightly on the lips. "Let's go."

Missy climbed onto his gelding without once complaining about having to straddle the horse and having her ankles showing. Jake was sure all of those concerns seemed trivial right now after almost being killed. Funny how a person's perspective changed after their life was threatened.

As they rode away from the cabin Jake said, "I'm sorry I didn't believe you from the start, Missy. It's just that I thought Devlin McCoy was my friend. I've known him for years and, well, I guess I misjudged him—and you."

"I shouldn't have expected you to trust me, Jake. We barely knew each other. And I lied to you about stowing away on the mail steamer," she said. "I was just so frightened. I didn't know what to do. And you were so handsome. I didn't want you to think badly of me."

"You think I'm handsome?" he asked, thrilled by this knowledge.

Missy glanced over her shoulder at him. Her face had reddened at the omission, yet she didn't look away. "How could I not?"

When she turned back around he sighed in her ear. "If you are trying to lure me into your web, it's too late. I'm there willingly and I don't plan on leaving anytime soon." He tightened his good arm around her and kicked the gelding into a faster pace.

He maneuvered the horse down a steep slope, in and

out of trees, but never entered an open meadow or road. Then they followed a small stream until it reached a large farm. Turning onto a plowed field, they rode straight for the large house that doubled as a hotel.

"Hello," Jake called out. "Fermer Walkley. Are you in there? It's Jake Gilbert."

The front door swung open. A tall, thin man with a large mustache and dressed in brown pants, suspenders, red flannel overshirt, and boots stepped outside. His eyes lit up and he smiled when he spotted Jake.

Jake slid off the horse and came over to shake Fermer's hand. "How you doing?"

"I'll be. I haven't seen you in some time." His gaze drifted to Missy. "And now I know why." Fermer grinned. "You two come inside. Jenny will be thrilled to have another woman to talk to."

"I'm sorry, we can't stay. Hopefully another time. I need you to do me a big favor." Jake relayed the incident at his cabin and asked Fermer to take the body to the marshal in Portland. He mentioned, too, that Kathleen O'Sullivan's horse was roaming somewhere on the mountain and to keep an eye out for it. Fermer agreed, but made Jake promise to return with Missy for a visit.

Jake remounted his gelding, holding his wounded arm in.

"You hurt?" Fermer asked.

"Yeah. The sorry bastard shot me in the shoulder," Jake said. "He won't repeat that mistake."

Fermer laughed as Jake and Missy rode away.

Jake felt Missy stiffen in his arms. "Is something the matter?"

"I just don't know how you can make jokes about killing a man," she said.

"He tried to murder me and you were next on his list," he said. "I hardly feel remorse for someone like that."

"I'm not used to all this killing," Missy said. "I see your point, but it seems wrong."

"I was defending myself. Kill or be killed," he said, unable to understand a woman's logic. "How can you come from a military background and not understand that?"

"I never had to see actual fighting," Missy said. "My father made sure of that."

"Your father sounds like he runs his family with a heavy hand," Jake said.

"Yes, indeed."

"So how did he react when you broke off your engagement to Surgeon Richard Barnes?" Just the man's name made Jake's stomach tighten.

She hesitated, and then said, "He was furious. That's why I didn't go home. My father had arranged the marriage. I knew Richard had feelings for me, but I didn't return them. I care for Richard, but not in the way a woman should if she intends to marry a man."

This news very much pleased Jake. He tightened his arm around her and listened as she continued on.

"It was my Uncle Irvin who gave me the courage to break off the engagement. I couldn't have done it without him."

"I'm beginning to like your uncle," Jake said.

"You would have loved him," Missy said, her voice filled with pride. "Despite all the horrors he saw during the Civil War, he was kind and gentle and caring. He kept telling me that one day I would find a man I would fall in love with, and that was the man I should marry."

"Am I that man?" Jake asked. His heart pounded in his chest waiting for her answer. He had never been on this side of the coin before, the one unsure of himself. He had always been the one in control, calling the shots, and normally leaving the woman disappointed. Now he finally knew what that felt like.

"Maybe," she said.

Jake smiled. She hadn't said no, and for now that was good enough for him.

"And what about you Jake? Shouldn't I know about your past?" she asked.

"Like what?"

"Tell me about your fiancée," she said. "What was her name?"

"Rachael."

"And what did she look like?" Missy asked.

"Like you."

She fell silent. After several long minutes she asked, "Is that why you're helping me? You think this is your way of helping Rachael?" She sounded hurt and a little betrayed.

"No. You might look like Rachael, but you are very different," he said.

"I hope for the better," she said.

"Much better. Rachael came from a wealthy family. Her parents spoiled her. Yet she was ambitious," he said.

"I don't follow."

"I told you I was a good lawyer. Well, I was the best,

and at one point I was destined for politics. She wanted to marry me because I would be powerful someday," he said, feeling a little angry inside.

"Did you love her?" Missy asked.

"I thought I did," Jake said. "But until I met you I didn't know what love was." He kissed the side of her head.

Missy didn't ask any more questions, and Jake hadn't planned on answering anything more. The last thing he wanted to talk about was why and how Rachael had died. He wished he could keep his sins in the past. Maybe someday people would let him.

Chapter Ten

Despite it being a little out of the way, Jake headed for a safe place, Mrs. O'Sullivan's boardinghouse. Not many people knew about his association with her, or that he owned the place. No one, not McCoy or another bounty hunter would think to look for them there.

Lights in the boardinghouse windows glowed, a comforting sight as they arrived just as the sun had set. Missy felt exhausted, hungry, and saddle sore. They stumbled into the kitchen where they found Mrs. O'Sullivan cleaning up. "Oh, thank the Lord, you found her," she said. "I was beginning to get worried."

Jake removed his poncho. His arm must have been throbbing, because he held it in, clenched fist to his chest.

"I need to take a look at that wound," Missy said.

"Wound?" Mrs. O'Sullivan exclaimed. "What happened?"

"A hired killer decided to use me as target practice," Jake said.

"Where is he now?" she asked.

"Slung over the back of a horse and heading for the marshal's office in Portland," Jake said.

"Let me get you two supper."

"We will both need a bath too," Jake said.

"I'll get going on that while you eat." Mrs. O'Sullivan stirred a pot on the stove. "It's still hot." She dished up two bowls full and set them on the table. Then she filled a basket with golden brown biscuits and placed it on the table with freshly churned butter and jam.

After Jake and Missy sat down and began to eat Jake said, "What do you have to wear tomorrow?" When she frowned he said, "I want you to dress nice, but conservative. We want to give the people of Astoria the impression that you are a proper woman."

"I am a proper woman," Missy said, feeling insulted by his comment.

"I know you are, but it doesn't matter what I think. What matters is what the public thinks, particularly the jury. They decide your fate. The jury will be respectable men in the community, and they're not going to want to convict a woman, especially if it means you getting hung. So we want you to look attractive, yet innocent. Luckily you have the face of an angel, which will work in our favor." He studied her. "Wear your hair back in a neat bun."

Anger began to boil inside Missy. "You don't think I'm innocent, do you?"

"Of course I do."

"Then why all the suggestions and comments about how I look?" Missy asked.

"Because this is a game of perception," Jake said. "It's like playing chess. You have to know the right moves to make." He took a bite of his stew, chewed and swallowed. "Let me ask you a question."

"Go ahead."

"How many times have you judged a person by their appearance?" he asked and waited for an answer.

"A few times," Missy said.

"You do it all the time," Jake said. "So do I. So does Mrs. O'Sullivan, and everyone else. It's human nature. So why not start working the jury the minute you step foot in Astoria?" He shrugged. "Makes sense to me."

"But I didn't commit this crime. Why should I have to convince them of that?" Missy felt the indignation of it all.

He looked at her incredulously. "Because you're going to be the one on trial. You're the one who is being charged with the crime. You know you're innocent. I know you're innocent. So why not convince the entire town of it? Like it or not, you have something to prove."

She expelled a sharp breath. "It's so unfair."

"Fair or not, it's the way it is." He shook his head. "You happened to be in the wrong place at the wrong time and caught by the wrong man."

"He didn't see me, you know."

Jake frowned. "Go on."

"When he stabbed my uncle I was in the shadows. I had come in the front of the store and heard McCoy and my uncle arguing, so I stopped and moved around a display and over to the wall where I could see who Uncle Irvin was arguing with. Devlin McCoy stabbed my uncle and ran out the back of the store, then returned later with his hired thugs, Morty and Moose." She struggled with tears in her eyes, and quickly blinked them away.

"How did he find out you were there?" Jake asked.

"He said he smelled my perfume," Missy said.

"Perfume?" Jake looked confused.

"My uncle gave it to me. It was from France."

"So what brought you to the store so late at night?"

"My uncle sent me a message to meet him there. I have no idea what it was about."

"Had he ever done that before?" Jake asked.

"No." She met his stare. She couldn't tell what was whirling around in his mind, only that something was.

"Tell me exactly what you overheard between your uncle and McCoy." Jake propped his elbows on the table, folded his hands, and leaned forward. When she didn't answer right away he said, "Think. This is very important."

Missy scratched her head, trying to search her brain. She shook her head and sighed in frustration. A moment later, her eyes widened and mouth dipped open. "Now I remember. I must have forgotten because of the shock."

"Remembered what?" Jake demanded.

"Something about documents." She bit her fingernail. "And Uncle Irvine called Mr. McCoy a Confederate slime."

Jake's head tipped back. "Are you sure?"

"Oh, my God. It's all coming back now." She rushed

on. "Yes. Uncle Irvine said he had gathered information about Mr. McCoy, and that—" Missy covered her hand over her mouth. She just realized why her uncle had been killed. At the time her mind had blocked it. But with Jake prompting her with all these questions it had triggered her memory.

"What, Missy? Tell me," Jake said.

She swallowed. "Uncle Irvine gathered information about McCoy that would put him behind bars or possibly get him hanged."

"Did your uncle tell you where he put this information?" Jake asked.

She shook her head. "No. But he told me to take the money and a key. He was insistent about the key."

"Did you get the key?" Jake asked.

"Yes."

"Where is it?" Jake looked as if he were ready to pounce on her.

"It's in my boot."

"Let me have it." He held his hand out, palm open.

Missy took off her right boot and found the key at the bottom. She handed it to Jake. "I don't know what it opens."

He stuffed the key in his pocket and leaned back in his chair. "Is there anything else you can remember that might be important?"

She thought for a moment. "Oh, yeah." She pointed her finger at him, jerking it up and down while she talked. "Uncle Irvine said he wanted the world to know that Colonel James something—Morgan never died." She shrugged.

Jake's eyes widened. "Are you sure about that name?"

"Yes. Why? Who is he?"

Before Jake could answer Mrs. O'Sullivan entered the room. "Well, one of you can start on their bath."

"Go ahead, Missy. I'm still eating," Jake said.

Missy stood, but paused. "Before McCoy stabbed my uncle he said his favorite thing to do to a Yank was to stab him, twist the knife, and listen to him squeal like a pig." Tears surfaced her eyes, but she didn't wipe them away. Instead she met Jake's eyes and said with pride, "My uncle never squealed." Missy held her head high as she walked to the back room to bathe.

Chapter Eleven

Jake wasn't sure if he had heard the name right or not. Col. James Huge Morgan was a murderer, thief, and savage. He ravaged women and slit the throats of children and the elderly. Jake remembered hearing rumors about the Colonel not really being dead. But they had only been rumors, nothing had materialized to substantiate them.

This man was dangerous, and if Devlin McCoy really was Morgan, then Missy was very lucky just to be alive. Things were starting to make sense. Now Jake knew why McCoy wanted *him* dead as well as Missy. McCoy knew of Jake's background, that he had been a lawyer, and a damn good one. McCoy probably started to get worried that Jake would take on Missy's case. McCoy needed Missy dead to ensure his secret. Jake could—and probably would—get Missy acquitted. McCoy couldn't take that chance, nor the chance of

Jake finding the documents to prove McCoy's true identity.

At least now Jake knew what he was dealing with. All he had to do was prove it. He pulled out the key Missy had given him and examined it. It looked like a key to a desk drawer, possibly in the store. But that seemed too easy to find. Irvine Douglas had to have been a clever man. After all, he did dig up the dirt on McCoy and that couldn't have been easy.

Jake finished eating. He opened the cupboard and pulled out a pint Mrs. O'Sullivan always kept on hand. He poured himself a drink, sipping the golden Irish whiskey. Mrs. O'Sullivan ambled into the room and took a seat across the table. Jake poured another glass and set it in front of her. "Your bath is ready."

Jake nodded. "Can you find Missy some suitable clothes?"

"I've got a room full of clothes left behind from our tenants," she said. "I'm sure one of those dresses will fit."

"It needs to be conservative," Jake said.

Mrs. O'Sullivan thought a minute. "There's a nice brown suit that was left here. I bet it would fit Missy."

"Sound perfect."

Mrs. O'Sullivan searched his face. "Are you going to be able to get her off?"

"I think so, but that's not what I'm worried about," Jake said.

She frowned.

"I'm not sure I'm going to be able to keep her alive," Jake admitted, "and that frightens me." His gaze dipped to the table top. "I don't know what I'd do without her." When Mrs. O'Sullivan touched his hand he glanced at her.

"Everything will turn out just fine," she said. "Then you'll marry this girl, have babies, and live happy for the rest of your lives."

He wished he could join in on her optimism. But then again Mrs. O'Sullivan had no idea who he was up against. If Devlin McCoy had fooled everyone for this many years, then that made the man cunning and very dangerous. How many other people had McCoy killed because they might have suspected he wasn't who he seemed to be? But somewhere Missy possessed evidence to hang the man, which put her in more danger than she could ever imagine.

Jake had arranged passage to take them down river on the pilot boat *Joseph Polutzer*. Jake was a little peeved because it took them almost as long as it would have had they taken a passenger steamer, because the pilot kept stopping at every town along the river. Once they reached the lower end of the Sanborn Docks, they hastened directly to the marshal's office, not far from the docks.

Jake whisked Missy inside and led her directly to the jail. Marshall Tanner sat at his desk reading a paper. As he glanced up his brows rose. "Miss Douglas. I'm so glad you decided to turn yourself in." He turned to Jake. "Mr. Gilbert. So you've returned with her. I'm sure you'll get paid handsomely for that."

Jake scowled. "I'm her lawyer. And I want to be reassured she will be protected at all hours of the day and night."

"I thought you were working for Mr. McCoy," Marshal Tanner said.

"Not since he hired a gunman to have Miss Douglas and myself killed," Jake said.

Marshall Tanner looked displeased, but not surprised by this news. "When did this happen and where?"

"Two days ago at my cabin on Mt. Hood," Jake explained.

"And where is this man now?" the marshal asked.

"In Portland. Dead."

"Who knows you're in town?"

Jake thought for a minute. "The pilot of the *Joseph Polutzer* and anyone who might have recognized us walking directly here from the docks."

"Thankfully the docks aren't far." The marshal turned to Missy. "How are you doing?"

"I'm doing my best."

He nodded. Gently, he gripped her elbow and guided her to an empty jail cell. Before he shut the door she asked, "May I have a Bible to read?"

"Of course. I'll have my wife come and talk to you too."

"Thank you." Missy sat down on the cot in the room and stared at the ground.

When the marshal returned to Jake he said, "I'll get my deputy to stand watch."

"I have things to do to prepare for this case. How soon will the circuit judge be able to get here?" Jake said.

"A week or two," Marshal Tanner said.

Jake departed and headed directly for Devlin McCoy's house. Once inside he waited in the parlor for McCoy to make his grand entrance. When Jake met the man's eyes, he noticed the startled look, followed by wariness.

"Surprised to see me, aren't you?" Jake asked. He kept his composure, his voice controlled.

Devlin quickly recovered and strolled over to pour himself a brandy. He guzzled it down in one gulp.

Jake tossed the bundle of cash on the table, hitting the brandy dispenser. "There's your blood money. The killer confessed that you had hired him to kill both Miss Douglas and myself."

Devlin wouldn't look at Jake.

"Why?"

"It was taking you so long to bring her back. I figured you had taken sides with her," Devlin said. "I told you how important this matter was to me."

"You shouldn't have done that," Jake said. "Because now you've made me your enemy. And you don't want me as your enemy."

Devlin laughed, and then glared at Jake. "You don't frighten me. You do anything, make one wrong move, and I'll have your past printed on the front page of every newspaper in the country."

"Go ahead. I did nothing wrong," Jake said.

"Your fiancée died at the hands of a man you defended," Devlin said. "You were run out of town. Hell, you were run out of half the country."

"I did my job. I was a defense lawyer and I defended a man charged with murder," Jake said. "The jury let him off, not me." How many times had Jake argued that point with himself in the past? But it wasn't until now that he started to believe it. He had wallowed in self-pity and guilt for so long. He was done with it. Done with taking the blame, done with punishing himself, and most of all done with other people condemning him for having done his job.

"I don't think the good citizens of Portland or Astoria would see it that way, especially after I put a certain twist on the story," Devlin said.

Jake stared at the man as if he was seeing him for the first time. Perhaps he was seeing McCoy—or Morgan—for the first time. He had seen a photograph of Colonel Morgan, taken at the time of the Civil War. Devlin might have aged a bit, but he had the same distinguished face, deep dark eyes, and tall frame. The mustache and peppered hair helped to hide his similarity to the clean-shaven Morgan, but he couldn't disguise his height or bone structure.

McCoy narrowed his glare at Jake. "You know, don't you?"

"Know what?" Jake asked, playing naive.

"I'd pay handsomely for those documents," McCoy said.

"Documents?" Jake asked, hoping the man would give himself away. "What documents are you referring to?"

McCoy just smiled. "Did you come by for any other reason?" He acted bored with the situation.

"Yes. I came to warn you. If you try to assassinate Miss Douglas, you'll be the one who hangs for murder," Jake said. "I've already informed the marshal about your involvement with the hired gun. If one hair on Miss Douglas' head is harmed, the marshal will be coming after you and you can forget about your political career."

"Are you defending her?" he asked.

"Yes. And I'm going to get her off," Jake said. "So your days are numbered and I'm counting them down." He pivoted around and exited the house. Jake heard something shatter inside the house. He was getting to McCoy. Good. That's what he wanted. Once he got the man on the stand, he would persecute him and relish every minute of it.

Jake's next stop was the wharf. The pier system in Astoria was the craziest he had ever seen. Instead of building the town on the hillside, they built piers straight out into the river. What they hadn't planned on was how to get from one pier to the next and one business to the next without returning to the beginning of each pier. So the business owners had built makeshift bridges from one pier to the next and it had been up to the business owners to maintain them. Some bridges were nothing more than planks, while others were sturdy and well constructed roads. Crossing between the piers in a storm or at night could find a person in the water, and that river proved to be mighty cold.

As Jake headed down Cass Street he saw the streets filled with people. Everywhere he looked buildings were going up and additional docks and wharfs were being erected. He strolled along the rough wooden roadway, and then turned left and walked along one of the connecting wooden streets, which ran from dock to dock. This one didn't have any railings, so Jake kept to the middle of the road, as far from the water as possible.

As Jake closed in on Irvine's store, near the corner of Cass and Squemocqha, pronounced Ska-mah-ka-way, dread started to fill him. The store looked as if it had been burned. Devlin had to have been behind this. No wonder he seemed fairly confident when Jake had spoken to him. And Devlin's lack of remorse over having Jake nearly killed, irked Jake. McCoy had acted as if his attempted murder on Jake had been no big deal. Well it was a big deal to Jake.

Jake stepped inside the Monitor Building where the first tri-weekly newspaper had just begun operations. He greeted the editor, Mr. DeWitt Ireland. "What happened next door?" Jake asked.

"Gave us quite a scare," Mr. Ireland said. "Luckily we were able to put it out before it damaged too much of the building or any of the surrounding buildings. Although I suspect most of the goods inside are ruined from smoke."

"Do you know how it started?" Jake asked.

"I'm not sure if it was vagrants starting a fire to keep warm, but someone started it on purpose. There was no accident about it," Mr. Ireland said. "I wrote an article in the newspaper, hoping someone would come forward to give me more information, but no one has."

"Is it safe to go inside?" Jake asked.

"As safe as any other business built on these long docks," Mr. Ireland said.

Jake turned to leave but the newspaperman paused him. "You new in town?" Mr. Ireland asked.

"I'm defending Miss Douglas," Jake said.

"The woman accused of murdering her uncle?"

"Yes."

"What did you say your name was?" Mr. Ireland asked.

"Jacob Gilbert."

Mr. Ireland tilted his head. "Where have I heard that name before?"

Jake shrugged. "I need to be on my way. Much obliged." Jake tipped his hat and exited the rickety and weather-worn old building. He opened the door to Irvine's store and entered. The store felt damp and smelled musty. The front windows allowed some light to see, but not enough. Jake found a match and lantern and used them to illuminate the room. He carried the lantern back and stepped behind the counter. Black charred scars ran up the walls. A coal circular area on the floor indicated where the fire had started.

Jake could smell the kerosene used to accelerate the fire. Why would vagrants use kerosene? No. This fire had been set deliberately. Mr. Ireland had assumed the same, but a newspaperman was as bound by the truth as a lawyer. They both needed facts to go forward with a story or a case.

Because Irvine had lived in the back of his store, Jake knew the documents might be here somewhere, but where? He ambled to the back room and opened the door. Irvine's bedroom had been torn apart, the bed turned over, dresser drawers yanked out and thrown about, and even his mattress ripped to shreds. The room reeked of desperation—McCoy's desperation.

Since McCoy asked Jake if he had the documents, that meant McCoy hadn't yet found them. Jake doubted he would find them here. Irvine went to a lot of trouble to dig up this dirt on McCoy. He wouldn't be stupid enough to put them where they could easily be found and destroyed.

Jake had about two weeks to find these documents. He hoped time wouldn't run out on him. Missy depended on him. Plus he'd promised to get her off. He still had tricks up his sleeve for courtroom theatrics that would turn the jury sympathetic toward Missy, but that was no guarantee. The documents were the only guarantee he had to prove Devlin McCoy killed Irvine Douglas.

Returning to the scene of the crime, Jake stared at the dry pool of blood. So where was the murder weapon? If Missy had stabbed her uncle, she most likely wouldn't have taken the weapon with her, especially if the murder had happened in the heat of the moment. People don't think logically when their emotions are all churned up.

Missy had mentioned an ivory-handled knife that McCoy owned. Jake couldn't recall Devlin ever using one, but that didn't mean he didn't own one. He probably dropped it into the river and it would be impossible to find now.

After leaving Irvine's General Store he stopped back in the newspaper office. "Sorry to bother you again," Jake said. "But I had a few questions for you."

"Shoot," Mr. Ireland said.

"The night Irvine Douglas was murdered were you here at the newspaper office?"

"I'm afraid not. It was a horrible night, rain pouring down, the wind whipping the rain. No. Only an idiot would have been out in that weather."

"Can I quote you on that?" Jake asked.

Mr. Ireland grinned. "Only if I can quote you about this trial."

"I'll give you an exclusive after it's over," Jake said. "Better yet, you can quote me right now when I say that Miss Douglas is completely innocent of this crime. Her uncle, Irvine Douglas, was already stabbed when she reached him."

"But you have a very credible eyewitness," Mr. Ireland said.

"Mr. McCoy must have had difficulty seeing that night. After all, you just said the weather was bad. It sounds like visibility was impossible."

"But the murder took place inside," Mr. Ireland pointed out.

"Yes, but Mr. McCoy said he saw the murder from outside the store. I'm presuming he saw something through the dirty windows from the front of the building," Jake said. He turned to glance out Ireland's own filthy windows. "How much can you see out of your own windows?"

Mr. Ireland smiled.

Jake turned to leave, but was halted by Mr. Ireland. "You know, for what it's worth Mr. Gilbert, I thought the newspapers and the people of Boston were unfair to you. I even wrote an article about it in the *Oregonian* when I was working there. I'm really glad to see you're returning to law. We need good lawyers like you."

Jake was stunned by Mr. Ireland's admission. No one had ever said they thought he had been treated unfairly. That little bit of support felt good. "Thank you." He didn't know what else to say.

"I'm not the only one who felt that way," Mr. Ireland said. "Many people in Portland did and still do."

Jake left the newspaper office feeling better than he had in years. Later that day, he paid Mr. Ireland another visit. This time he paid to put an article in the newspaper about Missy's volunteer work, her tending to the sick, helping at church functions, and giving what little she had to the needy. Then he questioned whether McCoy was really certain he'd seen Miss Douglas, a church-going, upstanding citizen of the community, commit the murder. If that didn't put pressure on McCoy, nothing would.

Missy sat in the dark jail cell fighting tears. She hadn't slept well on the cot, constantly looking for McCoy or his henchmen to burst in and shoot her. She had never felt more depressed in her life. Sometimes her head felt like it was spinning on top of her shoulders. Over and over she went through the scenario of how she got to this point. Her uncle had been murdered and here *she* sat in jail for it.

She stood up and rushed to the bars when Jake came into the room. He spoke with the deputy for a minute before he came over to her. She reached through the bars and clung to him. "Did you find anything?"

"Someone tried to burn your uncle's store down," Jake said.

"When?"

"I suspect shortly after his body had been discovered by authorities." He searched her face. "How are you holding up?"

She shrugged. She wasn't sure what happened to the soldier her father had raised her to be. The thought of getting hanged for a crime she didn't commit was beyond frightening.

"I brought you something," Jake said and handed her the newspaper. "I put an article in the newspaper about you. There's also an article about me. I was surprised to read it."

"What is that going to do?" Missy asked, confused.

"Get the public questioning your guilt," Jake said. "Chances are members of the jury will have read this article and start to doubt you did it."

Missy was amazed at how clever Jake was. She would never have thought of that tactic. "Now I see why you've never lost a case."

"I also visited McCoy. I warned him not to try any attempts on your life or he would be the one who hangs." He touched the side of her face. "He had better not lay a hand on you or I'll kill him."

"So what now? Do we wait?" she asked.

"You'll have to, but I have much more work to do. I've got to prepare for the case, figure out who I'll call as witnesses, and find angles in your defense. That kind of thing." He sighed. Dark circles rimmed his eyes. "I need to ask you something."

"What?"

"Do you have any idea where your uncle might have put those documents about McCoy?"

Missy dipped her gaze in thought. She rubbed her forehead as if that would help jog her memory. Then she said with a sigh, "No."

"Who did your uncle trust most in this town?" Jake asked.

Again, she contemplated the question. "Probably the marshal."

Jake tilted his head back, and then shook his head. "If he had given those documents to the marshal, McCoy would be arrested by now. No. Think. It's got to be someone else."

Then the thought hit her. Recognition dawned on her face.

"What is it?" Jake asked.

"The only other person my uncle would have given those papers to would be Richard," Missy said. "And Richard doesn't know that my uncle's been murdered or that I'm charged with the murder." She dropped her head forward and clunked it on the bar. "I can't believe this."

"When he gets back he'll get your note and know you're in trouble," Jake said.

"If he gets the message," she said, feeling incredibly gloom. "His nurse, Mrs. Lawton, didn't want Richard to see me again. And—"

"And what?" Jake asked, sounding like he didn't want to hear the rest.

"And I said some pretty mean things to her." She glanced at Jake. "Well, she made me so mad. She accused me of awful things." Missy felt her cheeks heat up.

"Are you certain your uncle would have given this information to Barnes?" Jake asked.

"His name is Richard," she said. "And yes. They're both military men." Her eyes widened. "Oh, my goodness."

"What?"

"That's what my uncle meant." She shook her head.

"You've lost me."

She licked her lips. "When I overheard the conversation between McCoy and my uncle, just before my uncle was stabbed, he said that the documents were in good hands and that if anything ever happened to my uncle the information would get out and McCoy would be exposed for the traitor he was."

"You didn't tell me this before," Jake said, sounding irritated.

"I didn't remember it until now," Missy said.

"So Irvine must have had a note attached to the documents that said they weren't to be opened unless he was dead," Jake surmised. "Why didn't your uncle take those documents to the marshal right away?"

Missy shrugged. "I don't know. Maybe he had just gotten all the information together. He did get something in the mail the day before he died."

Jake cursed under his breath.

"What is it?"

"There's no damn telegraph in this city," Jake said, "which means I will either have to track down Barnes or I'll have to send someone else to get him."

"Jake. He could be anywhere. Often he takes side trips on his way back to check on troops and tend to their medical needs." She sighed in frustration. "He could be anywhere in Oregon or the Washington Territory."

"I'll find him, Missy. Don't give up hope. I'm a tracker, remember? If anyone can find him, I can."

"But will you have enough time?" she asked, unable to keep the panic out of her voice.

"I hope so." He bent forward and kissed her on the lips. "I love you."

"I love you too."

Missy watched Jake speak to the deputy. He took one long look at her before he disappeared out the door. Suddenly, she felt empty. She sat down on her cot and opened the newspaper, immediately seeing her name. Reading the article, she smiled. He had made her sound like a saint. *My goodness, he really was a good lawyer.*

Yet that didn't give her any assurance that everything would turn out all right. Her fate would still be in the hands of the jurors. With McCoy looming, wanting nothing more than to see her hang, the odds were against her. Now all she could do was pray.

Chapter Twelve

Jake sought out the pilot of the *Joseph Polutzer* to see if he could get back up river as soon as possible. He had been surly with the man the day before and knew he would probably have to pay dearly to get the man to take him directly to the barracks. It wasn't hard to find the pilot in one of the saloons down on Astor Street. Jake packed a revolver with him, since this part of town was known for its gambling, drinking, bawdy houses, and shanghais.

The man was drunk but not plastered, so he hired him on the spot and they left immediately. By the time they reached the Vancouver Barracks it was afternoon. Jake wanted the pilot to wait for him, but the pilot refused. Jake headed straight for the medical center in the hopes of locating Surgeon Richard Barnes. Private Tom Pickering sat behind a desk, his head bent in consternation, studying papers. He looked up, his eyes widening when he saw Jake. "Mr. Gilbert. What can I do for you?"

Jake felt relieved that Mrs. Lawton wasn't around to hear their conversation. "Has Surgeon Barnes returned to the barracks?"

"I'm afraid he has come and gone," Tom said.

"Where'd he go?"

"Down river to a remote location on the Washington Territory side," Tom said. "It's called Pebble Peak. He goes there quite often to doctor the homesteaders."

"Did you give him the note from Miss Douglas?" Jake asked. Perhaps if he read that note he might be on his way to the abandon fort.

"Mrs. Lawton said she would handle that," Tom said.

"Did you read the note?"

Tom looked away, and then back. "Yes, but don't tell anyone. Surgeon Barnes would reprimand me if he knew I had done that."

"But he lets Mrs. Lawton read his messages?" Jake frowned.

"No. Mrs. Lawton makes sure Surgeon Barnes gets his mail," Tom explained.

Jake thought Tom was a bit naive about Mrs. Lawton not reading the good doctor's messages, but he said nothing about it. "Where may I find Mrs. Lawton?" Jake asked.

"In the infirmary," Tom said. "We've had several soldiers come down with dysentery and one with myalgia." Tom showed him the way through the infirmary doors and pointed to the older woman standing next to a bed.

Jake approached her. "May I speak with you Mrs. Lawton?"

"What is this about?" she asked.

"Let's just say it's a personal matter," Jake said.

"I have many patients who are ill here," she said. "I don't have time to take care of anyone's personal matters."

"Even if it's your own?" he asked.

She frowned and met his stare for several long seconds. With a jerk of her hand she motioned for him to follow her outside. Whirling to face him she asked, "What is this all about?"

"Did you give Surgeon Barnes the message Miss Douglas left for him?" Jake demanded.

She narrowed her glare at him. "Who are you?"

"I'm Jacob Gilbert. Miss Douglas's counsel."

"Is she in some kind of trouble?" Mrs. Lawton asked.

"Yes. And I need to speak with Surgeon Barnes. It's of the utmost importance."

She shook her head, and then crossed her meaty arms over her chest. "Leave him out of it. That woman is nothing but poison to him."

"Mrs. Lawton. I would like nothing better than to keep Surgeon Barnes away from Miss Douglas, but he has information that is vital to her case," Jake said. He hated having to reveal anything to this woman. The hatred this woman displayed for Missy was written all over the older woman's contorted face. "Did you give the message to Surgeon Barnes or not?"

Reluctantly she said, "No. And I won't apologize for

it. Richard is so much better off without that piece of fluff in his life."

Jake wanted to give this woman the lashing of her life, but he held his tongue. What good would it do? The woman didn't care about Missy's welfare or that her life had been in grave danger when she had waited for Barnes at the abandoned fort. Tipping his hat, he said, "Thank you for your time, ma'am." Returning to Tom, he asked, "Did Surgeon Barnes go out alone?"

"Yes. But you're going to have a heck of a time finding the man. "Pebble Peak is way out in the wilderness."

"I'll find him. Is there a place to rent a horse?" Jake asked.

"There's a livery stable just north of the barracks."

"There's one other thing I need you to do for me, Tom," Jake said. "This is confidential and most urgent. I don't want you letting anyone else handle this matter, but you."

Tom furrowed his thin brows. "What is it?"

"I need you to send a telegram to Surgeon John Edgar Douglas," Jake said. He scribbled the message, *Urgent! Come to Astoria immediately. Daughter being tried for murder of uncle.* He sighed it, *Jacob Gilbert, Attorney at Law.*

Tom glanced at the message, and then at Jake.

"I'd appreciate it if you would keep this confidential," Jake said.

"Of course, sir. I'll get on this right away," Tom said, giving Jake a salute.

"Room and board are on me next time you're in

Portland," Jake said and departed. He rented a horse and saddle, stopped at a general store for a few supplies, and went on his way, following the Columbia River heading northwest. Night would fall before he got close to Pebble Peak, even if he rode at a fast pace. He made camp outside under a large fir tree, using cut tree limbs for warmth, along with the blanket he purchased. He ate dried meat and fruit for supper and drank water from a canteen.

Jake slept little through the night. Too many thoughts kept him awake, like Missy's fate, finding Barnes, and bringing Barnes back into Missy's life. The idea didn't appeal to him at all, but he figured Barnes would insist on coming back to Astoria with him once he heard the entire story.

The morning brought with it wind and mist, making travel uncomfortable. Jake buttoned his coat and lowered his hat. He worried that the weather would wash and blow away the doctor's tracks before he reached Pebble Peak. A track was a temporary thing, existing for a relatively brief time on the ground where the wind could push it flat, rain could wash it away, and nature did its best to steal the rest of the traces away.

He kept his pace brisk and started looking for tracks as he neared the area. Once he found recent horse tracks, possibly accompanied by a man's shoe, he would make quick progress. It was just finding the tracks in the first place.

Jake was always fascinated by how a track could tell so much about a person or creature. When an animal's tracks stopped, he could still see how it paused, how it rested its body, or what activity it might have been doing. The tracks were impressions of the animal, be it man or beast. They were a mystery, not that much different from solving a case. Perhaps that was why he took to both becoming a lawyer and a tracker.

Scouring the area, Jake searched the woods and grassy knolls. Half the morning went by before he found tracks. Indian Joe could track at a dead run, but it would take Jake many more years before he could move that quickly. Frustrated, he knew the minutes were ticking away.

Once Jake reached an open area, he moved much faster, and even mounted his horse and followed on horseback. The smell of smoke filled the air, causing him to glance around. He rode up to the ridge of an open hill to get a better view. Just on the other side of the meadow stood a small house, its chimney spewing smoke.

Jake began to get an uneasy feeling as he neared. In the corral was an army steed. The horse whinnied and Jake's gelding returned the sound. Just as he reached the house, the front door whipped open. A tall, thin man wearing a military uniform stood on the doorstep with a pistol in hand. He raised the gun and pointed it at Jake.

"I'm looking for Surgeon Richard Barnes," Jake said.

"You found him," Richard said. "State your business."

"I'm Jacob Gilbert. I'm an attorney for Melissa Douglas. She's in trouble and you may be the only one who can help her," Jake said, cringing at the last few words he forced out of his mouth.

Richard glanced behind him into the house, said a few words to someone in there, and then shut the door behind him. He met Jake by the hitching post just as Jake dismounted. "Did Missy—I mean Miss Douglas send for me?"

Jake's gut tightened. The good old doc looked way too hopeful. "Sort of." Jake glanced around the yard. "Is there somewhere else we can talk, rather than out here?"

"Let's talk in the barn," Richard said.

As they walked past the corral, Jake glanced over his shoulder to find a young woman—oddly enough with coal black hair and about Missy's age—and a young boy around two-years-old standing on the porch watching them. Jake took another look at the boy. There was no mistake. He was Richard Barnes's son. Which meant Barnes had relations with this woman while he had been courting Missy. Jake wondered how many other families the doctor might have up and down the Columbia River. He instantly hated the man even more.

Once inside the barn, the doctor gave Jake his undivided attention. "What's this all about?"

Jake said, "Miss Douglas's uncle, Irvine Douglas, was murdered, and Miss Douglas is being accused of the murder."

The doctor looked in shock. "Missy wouldn't hurt a fly. I've known her all her life, since she was a baby. Who's accusing her of this?"

This close, Jake was amazed at how much older the doctor was than Missy. He had to be in his early fifties. The idea of this old man touching Missy with his filthy hands made Jake's fists ball up tight and his knuckles turn white. "It's a long story, one I don't have time to get into. I need to get documents from you. They could clear Miss Douglas of all wrongdoing."

"Documents?" Barnes seemed genuinely confused.

Dread began to rush into Jake's gut. He pushed on. "Did Irvine Douglas at any time in the past give you documents to hold for him?"

The doctor scratched his balding head. "He might have, a long time ago. I can't recall."

"You'd better recall, because Miss Douglas's life depends on it," Jake said.

"I must return to Astoria with you," Richard said. "Once I'm there, I'm sure it will jog my memory."

The last thing Jake wanted was to have the doctor come back and reunite him with Missy. When people got desperate they did things they normally wouldn't do. Missy might feel more protected by Barnes, especially since he had to be close to her father's age. She might mistake that comfort for love and try to rekindle their romance.

"If you return with me, you must understand that Miss Douglas is my client," Jake said. "I don't want you interfering in her case."

Richard posed an indignant stance. "Missy is very dear to my heart. I will do whatever I have to, to help her."

Jake shook his head. "Not on my time." Jake turned and walked away.

Richard jogged to catch up to him. "Okay. You win. But if she asks for my help I will give it to her."

Jake shrugged. He figured the man would be interfering and difficult. His instinct told him so.

"Let me take care of a few things in the house," Richard said, acting a little uncomfortable for the first time.

Jake mounted and waited. He heard raised voices inside, followed by a door slamming. A few minutes later Richard was on the front porch with the small boy. He patted the top of the child's head. "Take care of your mother," Richard said. Minutes later the doctor had his mount bridled and saddled.

As they rode away Richard said, "The first thing we need to do is send a telegram to Surgeon John Edgar Douglas, Missy's father."

"I've done that already," Jake said.

"Good." Richard darted several glances at Jake before he said, "Uh—we don't have to mention anything to Miss Douglas about—" he jerked his head back toward the cabin. "There's no reason she needs to know about my—uh—sister."

Jake laughed out loud. "Is that what you call her? So I suppose that young boy, who is the spitting image of you, is your nephew?"

Richard's face reddened. "That whole thing happened quite by accident."

"They always do, don't they?" Jake said, feeling no sympathy for the man, only for the woman and child. "How old's the child?"

"Almost two," Richard said.

"So you must have been seeing this woman while you were courting Miss Douglas?"

Richard's eyes flared and the muscle in his jaw flexed. "Just who the hell did you say you were?"

"Jacob Gilbert, Attorney at Law. Oh, yes. Did I mention that Miss Douglas and I are engaged to be married once this court case is over with?"

Richard's face flamed red. "Married. This must be a joke."

Jake shook his head. "It's no joke. Missy has agreed to marry me."

"How long have you known her?" he demanded.

"Not long," Jake admitted.

"She's not thinking straight. And how could she with everything going on?" Richard said, his eyes now narrowed in slits. "I'll talk some sense into her."

Jake halted his horse, causing Richard's mount to pause. "Miss Douglas is a lot better off with me than she would have been with you. Don't interfere in our relationship. You don't want me as your enemy."

"Is that a threat?" Richard asked.

Jake kicked his gelding forward. "Take it however you want. I'm just warning you now."

They rode for the next hour in silence. Jake had so many things going through his mind about the case, especially having to do with the documents. If Richard didn't have them, then who did? Did they even exist? Could Irvine have been threatening McCoy with imaginary proof just to scare him? And if that were true, that meant Irvine had been murdered for no reason at all.

Jake hoped the documents did exist. He wanted the truth to come out about Col. Morgan—a man about as evil as one could get, filled with hatred and deceit. The sooner that man was hung for his crimes the better.

"I know a shortcut to the river," Richard said. "We can catch a steamer and board our horses there." He led the way down the hillside through a wooded path.

Once they reached the small town, Jake hired a

young man to return his horse back to the livery. That way he wouldn't have to come back this way to do it. Since they had several hours to wait before the steamer arrived, they ate at the only restaurant in town, which also served as the local saloon. Jake had the best chicken pot pie he had ever tasted. When the cook came out to their table with an apple strudel dessert that tasted beyond belief he said, "I own the Palace Hotel in Portland. Have you ever heard of it?"

"Of course," she said.

"You ever get tired of working here, you've got a job in my hotel," Jake said to the cook. He introduced himself and asked for her name.

When she walked away Richard said, "You own the Palace Hotel?"

"That's what I said," Jake said.

"That's a pretty fancy place. What else do you do?" Richard sounded like a concerned father.

"If you're asking if I can take care of Missy, the answer is yes," Jake said. "She won't want for anything."

"So that's the attraction," Richard said.

Jake smiled, but he wasn't humored. "Miss Douglas doesn't even know I own anything in town. She thinks I make my living tracking people and animals."

"Ah, yes. I read about you, rescuing poor souls who've lost their way." Richard took a sip of his coffee.

Jake really hated this man.

Richard set his elbows on the table and shook his finger at Jake while he talked. "And if I recall you're known for something else, much bigger. Something that happened back in Boston, wasn't it?"

"I've already told Missy about that part of my past," Jake said, "so don't try and blackmail me."

With much more confidence Richard said, "Yes, well, of course you've told Missy. And being the forgiving woman she is she has overlooked your . . . mistakes. But I assure you her father won't."

Jake laughed. "So what would her father think about your sister and nephew?"

Richard's cocky grin faded. "You could never prove that's my child."

"He looks exactly like you," Jake said. "What kind of man won't take responsibility for his own child? Come on. Be a man. Marry the woman and give the child your name."

Richard leaned back in his chair and sighed. "Advice coming from a man who was run out of town." He took another sip of his coffee. "You know I was actually there in Boston during the trial. I read about the case everyday in the newspaper. You had quite a future." He sucked in a breath. "And Miss Rachael Hancock. What a beauty. She strikes a great resemblance to Missy, doesn't she?"

With fists knotted at his sides, Jake glared at the obnoxious man. "Come on, Barnes, just spit it out. Don't play games with me. If you want to say something, then say it."

Richard leaned forward on the table, his face contorted in anger and eyes piercing. "Okay I will. You are not good enough for the likes of Missy. And I refuse to see her married to you."

"This has nothing to do with my past," Jake said

calmly. "You don't want to see Missy married to any other man but you." Jake leaned forward on the table, his face inches from Barnes'. He lowered his voice to a whisper, "And I refuse to see her married to you." He sat back in his chair and studied the doctor. For a surgeon, Jake had expected the doctor to have more patience and control of his emotions.

Richard flopped back in his chair. "I say we let her father decide."

"You already tried that, remember? Missy broke off your engagement," Jake said, grinning.

"You are despicable," Richard hissed.

"No more than you," Jake said, holding the man's glare. He set his napkin beside his plate and stood. Dropping money on the table to pay for his meal, he strolled out of the building. Outside the air smelled fresh and clean. He could see the steamer approaching and made his way down to the dock to wait to board.

Chapter Thirteen

Minutes later Richard joined him, but refused to speak to Jake. While on board the *Emma Stewart* Jake picked up a newspaper. He was stunned to read that the circuit judge would be arriving in Astoria within days and wanted to get the case started immediately. This would give him little time to prepare. He wrote down a list of names of potential witnesses he might call, including McCoy.

Richard sat on the other side of the boat from Jake, keeping to himself. They didn't meet up until they departed the ship and headed on foot to the jail. As they approached City Hall, Richard increased his pace up the steep hill, and darted inside the building.

By the time Jake reached the jail, Richard stood at the cell, his hands through the bars cupping Missy's face. Jake didn't like the man touching Missy at all, but kept his opinion to himself.

"Missy," Richard said. "Why didn't you come to *me* when all of this happened?"

"I did Richard," she said. "I sent you several messages. I even went to the barracks and left you a note."

"I never received any message from you," Richard said. "I'll have that private court marshaled."

"I believe you need to talk to your nurse, Mrs. Lawton," Jake said. "She has your messages from Missy and refuses to give them to you."

"How do you know this?" Richard said in a challenging fashion.

"She told me," Jake said simply.

"This is a ridiculous accusation," Richard said, his voice rising. "Mrs. Lawton has been loyal to me for years. She would never do such a thing."

Missy gripped Richard's arm. "Do you have the documents?"

He shook his head. "I don't believe your uncle gave me any documents. Not that I remember."

Missy looked as if someone had punched her in the gut. "He had to have. You're the only other person I could think of he would trust."

"There must be someone else," Jake said. "Think, Missy."

"Don't pressure her," Richard said. "She's under enough strain without you harping on her."

"These documents will set her free," Jake said. "We need them. Her court case begins in a few days."

"Marshal Tanner told me the circuit judge will be here soon. I hoped you would get back in time," Missy said, addressing Jake.

Jake wanted to touch Missy, hold and kiss her, but Barnes wouldn't budge. "Come here," Jake said, reaching through the bars. She moved down to him. When he touched the side of her face she closed her eyes. Then tears began to flow. Jake tried to hug her, but the bars were in the way.

"Now look what you've done," Richard said. "You made her cry."

Jake tilted Missy's chin up and kissed her lightly on the lips. Sure, he did it to make Richard mad and it had worked.

"Missy," Richard said, "let me get you another lawyer, a more competent one."

She shook her head. "No. I want Jake. He's the best."

"I suppose *he* told you that," Richard said.

"He has never lost a case," Missy said.

Jake liked how she sounded like she was bragging about him, especially to this nitwit doctor.

"But—"

"Richard, no," Missy said. "I want Jake to defend me."

Richard's head tipped back as if she had slapped him in the face. Jake suspected Missy had never taken that tone with him before. Jake couldn't help but grin.

"Have you had any visitors?" Jake asked.

"Just Mrs. Tanner," Missy said. "And if you're asking me if McCoy has stopped by the answer is no. Thank goodness."

"Who's McCoy?" Richard asked.

"He's the man accusing me of committing this murder, when in fact, *he* murdered my uncle," she said. She crossed her arms over her chest.

"I'll just have a talk with this man," Richard said.

"No you won't." Jake frowned. "I don't want you or anyone Missy knows to go see that man. He's dangerous."

"I know what I'm doing," Richard said.

Jake jabbed a finger in the air at him. "You do anything to damage this case and I'll have you demoted to private."

"I'm shaking in my boots," Richard said sarcastically.

"Would you two stop it?" Missy said. "I don't want two men I love fighting."

Richard and Jake glared at each other before they returned their attention to Missy.

Marshal Tanner stepped into the room and motioned Jake over. "I hate to tell you this, but word around town is that McCoy has offered to pay jurors handsomely if they vote to convict Miss Douglas."

Jake swore under his breath. He hoped McCoy wouldn't resort to such tactics, but wasn't surprised he had. Even though it showed signs of desperation on McCoy's part, jurys could be bought without trouble. Only one or two jurors could convince the rest of the group to vote their way. "You didn't tell Miss Douglas, did you?"

"No." Marshal Tanner looked worried.

"Is there anything you can do about this?" Jake asked, knowing the answer.

"Not without proof," Marshal Tanner said.

"Why are jurors being selected so soon?" Jake asked. "Normally the court waits for the judge to get here."

"Because this case is causing such a sensation,"

Marshal Tanner said. "A beautiful woman accused of murder. Her word against a rich and powerful man running for political office. People eat this kind of thing up."

Unfortunately, it was at Missy's expense. "I'm going to call you as a character witness," Jake said to the marshal.

"That's fine."

Jake stepped back over to Missy and Richard. Richard fell silent when Jake approached, but he heard bits and pieces of the good old doc trying to convince Missy to find another lawyer. Jake interrupted. "I'll be back later to check on you."

Missy nodded.

"Try and get some rest," Jake said, and then glared at Richard. But Richard didn't leave.

As Jake departed, he quietly asked Marshal Tanner to limit Richard's visit and any future visits with Missy. The marshal agreed. Jake left the jail and returned to his hotel room. He had much to do to prepare and in a much shorter period of time than he had planned. He couldn't shake this nagging feeling about this case and the fate of Missy Douglas.

Missy took a deep breath as Marshal Tanner and Jake led her from the jail to the courtroom. Jake remained by her side the entire way. The courthouse had people lined up outside hoping to get in to see the trial. With sweaty palms and a shaking body, Missy wove her way through the crowds doing her best to ignore the taunting and jeering by some of the people. But she had to admit that many of the local townspeople, the ones who knew her, supported her and voiced their support as she scurried by them.

Inside, the courtroom had a limited number of benches for the spectators and two tables with two chairs at each table that stood in front of a tall bench. Missy had never been inside a courtroom before and the scene before her was intimidating. Richard had already seated himself directly behind her and gave her a reassuring nod before she sat down and faced the judge.

She felt as if she was in a dream. She tried to focus on the judge and jurors like Jake had told her to, making eye contact with them. A few of the men she had seen in church, but that didn't give her much comfort. A few looked like fishermen and cannery workers, but three men she worried about. One owned a brothel in town and the other two looked like sailors. Missy knew exactly which jurors would pose obstacles for her.

The judge pounded a gavel on the podium to gain everyone's attention. He had a white head of hair and wore a black flowing gown. The glasses he wore and the wrinkles on his face indicated he had been a judge for many years. He was announced as Judge Ayers and spoke in a no-nonsense tone. He told the courtroom that he would not tolerate outbursts or noise from the gallery. If any occurred, then he would clear the room and proceed with the case with only the prosecution, defense, and jury. His words quieted the crowd down.

The case began with opening statements. Missy smiled when Jake spouted her virtues to the jury. He seemed so confident he would prove her innocence. Watching the jurors, she could tell he had a great effect on many of them, although the sailors and the owner of the brothel looked anything but impressed.

Missy glanced over at the prosecutor, Fredrick Billings, an older man with graying hair and short stature. She had seen him in church on many occasions and had even brought supper over to him and his family when his wife fell sick. She guessed none of that mattered now. He would do his best to convict her. Glancing over her shoulder, Missy scanned the crowd for his wife. She found her sitting in the very back. Meeting her stare, Missy watched as the other woman glimpsed away. She began to feel more alone than ever. People whom she'd met in church or she'd helped seemed to be turning their backs on her.

She looked forward as Jake called Surgeon Richard Barnes to the stand. Watching Jake, she was amazed at how he operated in the courtroom. He was in his element, mesmerizing the jury and audience, like an actor on stage.

"Doctor Barnes," Jake said.

"I prefer to be called Surgeon Barnes," Richard said.

Jake seemed unaffected by Richard's comment. "Surgeon Barnes. How long have you known Miss Douglas?"

"Since she was born," he said, and smiled.

"Twenty-two years, then, is that correct?" Jake asked.

"Yes."

"And in that time have you ever known her to be a violent person?"

"No. In fact, Miss Douglas is the most gentle and caring woman I've ever met," Richard said, glancing at Missy with love in his eyes.

"And you have seen her with her uncle, have you not?" Jake asked.

"Yes. She took care of her uncle," Richard said.

"Can you give us examples of how she cared for her uncle?"

"In many ways. She helped him at his store. She always walked him to and from church, she mended his clothes, cooked him meals." Richard started to get on a role, speaking his mind. "Miss Douglas would never harm her uncle in any way. She loved him dearly." He turned to address the jury. "The idea that she would murder anyone, let alone her own uncle, is outrageous!" Richard's face turned red. "If you knew her you would know that she couldn't hurt a fly. She has helped people, tended to the sick and poor her entire life. She has worked in the hospital with her father, Surgeon John Edgar Douglas, and her mother, a nurse." He stood and shook his finger in the air like a preacher on the pulpit. "The man who thinks he saw her harm her uncle is mistaken. He has to be. Miss Douglas is a proper woman. To convict her would be a sin."

The judge pounded the gavel. "Surgeon Barnes. Please sit down."

"No further questions," Jake said.

Richard slowly sank into his chair.

Fredrick Billings, the prosecutor, pushed out of his chair and paced in front of the jury in a dramatic fashion, his hands behind his back, his head bent in thought. Then he paused in front of Richard and asked, "Were you and Miss Douglas engaged to be married?"

"Yes."

"Were you in love with her?" he asked.

"Yes."

"Are you still in love with her?"

"To know Miss Douglas is to love her," Richard said.

"So would you say you are biased when it comes to Miss Douglas?" Billings asked.

Richard opened his mouth, but then shut it. He hesitated, not knowing how to answer the question.

"Answer the question, Surgeon Barnes," Billings said.

"I might be a little biased, but—"

"No further questions."

Jake stood and halted Richard before he could get off the stand. "Surgeon Barnes. Would you say that your opinion about Miss Douglas is shared by people who don't know her as well?"

"Yes," Richard said.

"Objection, Your Honor," Billings said. "He's asking the witness for his own opinion."

The judge nodded his agreement. "Mr. Gilbert, either ask another question or let the witness step down."

Missy could tell by Jake's expression that he had expected the prosecutor and judge to say that. "Yes, Your Honor. Surgeon Barnes, have you ever heard, say someone at the barracks—someone unrelated to Miss Douglas—ever comment on her character?"

"There're too many people to list," Richard said.

"Just give me a few examples," Jake said.

"Sargeant George Sheffield said he was impressed by her dedication to others. His wife, Henrietta Sheffield said Miss Douglas was the kindest person she had ever met," Richard said. He gave two more examples before Jake stopped him.

"Thank you Surgeon Barnes." Jake waited for Richard to return to the gallery. Richard touched Missy on the shoulder, giving her a reassuring squeeze before he sat down. She smiled at him, touched by how he had defended her.

Jake then called Marshal Tanner to the stand, and then his wife, and Mrs. Baker. All three gave Missy glowing reports of her charity work and told the jury they did not believe she could have possibly killed her uncle. Missy could tell the jury seemed to listen to the marshal's comments closely. She hoped he had helped. The prosecutor hardly questioned the marshal, and only threw out a few questions to his wife and Mrs. Baker.

Before the star witness, Devlin McCoy, could take the stand, the court was adjourned for the day and would reconvene the following morning at 8:00. Jake walked with Missy back to the jailhouse, but didn't stay long with her. Once again, she was left all alone to ponder the case and worry about the outcome.

Jake returned to his room and sat down at the table. He jotted down the questions he intended to pound McCoy with. While the prosecutor questioned Richard, Marshal Tanner, and his wife, he studied the jurors. He could tell many of them had been swayed in Missy's favor by what the witnesses had said about her, but he worried about two of the jurors. They looked like seasoned sailors who could be easily bought. Those two men appeared bored with the entire procedure, as if they had already made up their minds to convict her.

Sighing, he leaned back in his chair. He had dealt with

many juries before, but none of them had been bought off, at least none that Jake knew of. He rubbed his clean-shaven jaw and stared blindly at the wall. What could he do about those jurors? At the moment nothing, which brought him back to the same dilemma: He needed those documents Irvine had collected to nail McCoy. Once he found them this case would be dropped.

But where were they?

He pulled out the key and rolled it between his thumb and index finger. What do you belong to? A box? A desk? A safe? What? How could a woman's fate lie in this small metal object? He set it on the table.

A knock at the door brought Jake out of his thoughts. He opened the door to find a maid carrying a tray with his supper on it. He motioned for her to put the tray on the table. After she set it down she said, "That's a strange key for a single man to be carrying around with him." She scurried to the door. Before she could leave Jake asked, "What do you mean?"

She nodded to the key. "Only that that key looks like the one I use to lock up my jewelry box." She curtsied and quickly shut the door.

Jake stared at the closed door. Jewelry box? But he had looked in Missy's jewelry box and never found any documents, only a few pieces of jewelry. He had to admit, though, that he hadn't examined the box very thoroughly.

He glanced outside the window. Nighttime had settled down on them and it was late into the evening. After court tomorrow he would go back to Mrs. Baker's boarding-house and check through Missy's belongings. Maybe he had missed something—something very important.

Sitting back down at the table, he ate his supper while he continued preparing for tomorrow's key witness. Missy's life depended on how he did in the cross-examination. He didn't want to blow it. If he did, it could mean her life.

Chapter Fourteen

The courtroom hummed as Jake guided Missy to her chair. He could feel her shaking. She knew how important today would be, just as he did. Giving her a reassuring smile, he patted her hand. "Be strong," he whispered. She nodded.

As the prosecution called Devlin McCoy to the stand and began questioning him, Jake wrote down many notes. McCoy had so many holes in his story, and Jake intended to pounce on every one of them. At long last it was his time to cross-examine.

He straightened his suit as he approached McCoy. "Mr. McCoy," Jake said, "you said you were taking an evening stroll when you came upon two people arguing. Is that correct?"

"Yes."

"What kind of night was it?" Jake asked.

Devlin shrugged. "I can't recall."

Ignoring his response, Jake said, "Wasn't it in fact a

miserable, rainy night with high winds? Wasn't it rain-
ing so hard that no one else was on the street that
night?"

Devlin shook his head. "I can't recall."

Jake frowned. "You can't recall what the weather
was like, yet you insist you recall seeing Miss Douglas
murder her uncle. Don't you find that strange?"

"No." Devlin's arrogant attitude slipped a little as
Jake's questions annoyed the man.

Jake suppressed a grin. He wanted to get Devlin irritated to the point where the man would lose his temper.
"I have a dozen people I can call to the stand who will
testify that the weather that night was miserable.
Should I call everyone of them, just to refresh your
memory?"

"Call whomever you like. I saw what I saw, no matter what the weather was like," Devlin said, grinning.

"And where did you see this murder?"

Devlin frowned.

"Let me make myself clearer. Were you outside
looking in when you saw this murder? Or had you gone
inside and actually witnessed the murder?"

"I saw it from outside, but I did go inside and saw
Miss Douglas standing over the victim with a knife in
her hand."

"That's a lie and you know it!" Missy yelled, jumping to her feet.

The judge hammered his gavel and reprimanded
Missy. Jake rushed over to her and whispered, "You
need to keep quiet. He's lying, but you have to let me
prove it without any more outbursts. Okay?"

She reluctantly agreed and plopped back into her chair.

He returned to Devlin on the stand. "So where were we, Mr. McCoy? Oh, yes, you were saying you saw the defendant standing over her uncle with the weapon in her hand. So what did the weapon look like?"

"A knife."

"Was it a large knife, small knife, did the knife have any kind of distinguishing features?" he asked.

Devlin shrugged. "I think it had a white handle, but I can't be sure."

Jake smiled. He was hoping McCoy would be vague. "So you're telling me that you can't be sure what the knife looked like, yet from outside on a stormy night you could be sure that you saw Miss Douglas stab her uncle?"

Devlin's face reddened.

Jake continued without giving McCoy a chance to reply. "When you were looking in from outside, how clean were the windows of the store?"

Devlin shrugged again.

"You don't recall?" Jake said.

"They were clean enough to see through them," Devlin said.

"Hmm. Really now. Because I went down there just the other day and they were so dirty from the weather that I couldn't see to the front of the store." He addressed the jury, knowing some of them owned stores on the piers. "How often do you clean your windows around here? With as much wind and rain that you receive, you have to clean them often, don't you?"

Some of the jurors nodded. "Irvine Douglas hadn't cleaned his in months if not years."

McCoy began to get upset. Anger turned his face and neck red. "I saw that woman stab her uncle in his store."

Jake whirled around. "Mr. McCoy. Why were you taking a stroll on a very stormy night?"

"I always take a stroll after supper," he said.

"Even in bad weather?" Jake asked.

"Yes," he said.

"Then let me pose another question to you," Jake said. "Your home sits up on a hill, overlooking downtown Astoria and the Columbia River, does it not?"

"Yes."

"It occupies a full city block too. Right?"

"Yes."

"Would you say your home is in the finer part of Astoria?" Jake asked.

"Yes, but what's that got to do with anything?"

Jake scratched his head. "Because I can't figure out why an affluent man such as yourself would be taking a stroll—on a stormy night—in one of the most run down parts of town." He made eye contact with the jurors, and then back to Devlin. "Why not take a stroll near your home? Especially when it was such bad weather?"

Again, Devlin's face reddened. Jake could tell the man hadn't thought this one through. Devlin shook his head. "I guess I started walking and wasn't really looking where I was going."

"And you ended up far out on the pier?" Jake asked incredulously. "Sounds strange to me."

"I am running for political office," Devlin said. "I wanted to talk to the other kinds of people in this town."

"Other kinds of people?" Jake asked. He turned to the jury. "It appears Mr. McCoy believes there are several classes of people in the good town of Astoria."

"Come now, Counselor, we all know there are people who make the laws and those who live by them," Devlin said.

"And you believe you don't have to live by the rules?" Jake asked.

Devlin narrowed his glare at Jake. "You seem to read a lot into what I say."

"No. I'm just trying to figure out what you're saying," Jake said, and then rushed on. "So you said that you were down at Irvine Douglas' shop to talk to the 'other' people in town." He shrugged. "How can that be when no one apparently, but you, was out that night? Everyone else was snuggled inside a warm home or building."

At this Devlin remained tight-lipped.

"Your Honor, will you instruct the witness to answer the question?" Jake asked.

"Answer the question, Mr. McCoy," Judge Ayers said.

The look on Devlin's face was nothing but total contempt for Jake. "Despite the weather conditions there were other people out and about."

"Who?"

"Two sailors."

"Do they have names?" Jake asked.

"Morty Fenfield and Moose Tuchy." Devlin formed a derisive smile.

"Don't those two sailors work for you?"

"On occasion."

"So who else did you meet?" Jake asked. "Because I asked owners of stores near Irvine Douglas' store, and all of them told me they had closed shop and gone home because of the bad weather."

"I don't know their names," Devlin snapped. "That's why I was down there to reach out to the voting public."

"Tell us what they looked like, then," Jake said. When Devlin said nothing Jake continued. "Were they tall, short, male, female?"

"I can't remember."

"You can't remember what the people looked like you talked to. You can't remember what the weather was like that night." He lifted his brows in doubt. "You can't remember much, can you Mr. McCoy? Yet you claim you remember seeing Miss Douglas—a good law-abiding citizen of Astoria, a woman who loved her uncle dearly and has given to this community in many ways—murder her uncle."

"Yes."

Jake shook his head. "You know what I think, Mr. McCoy?"

"I don't really care what you think," he spat.

"Well, I'm going to tell you anyway." Jake smiled, kept a steady stare on Devlin and continued, "I think you purposefully went down to see Irvine Douglas about something, perhaps some personal business. You two got into a heated conversation and you drew a knife, the ivory one you own, and stabbed him. I think you are the murderer, Mr. McCoy, and that Miss Douglas happened to come in at the wrong time. You thought, and even told her, that because you are a rich and powerful man, that no one would believe her story, only yours." The crowd gasped.

"You can't prove any of that," Devlin said.

"Interestingly you said I can't prove it. Shouldn't you be saying that my account of what happened isn't true?" He walked around to stand on the other side of Devlin, closer to the jurors. "I contend that I have as much proof that you killed Irvine Douglas as you and the prosecutor have that Miss Douglas did it. Because it comes down to your word against hers. There's no real proof on either side, is there?"

A light perspiration appeared on Devlin's forehead for the first time. He patted his head with a handkerchief.

"Do you have any other proof, other than your being a witness, that can prove Miss Douglas killed her uncle?" When Devlin said nothing he raised his voice. "Did you hear the question Mr. McCoy? Do you have any other proof?"

"My word should be all the proof you need," Devlin said in an arrogant manner. "I'm a rich and influential man in this town. I'm running for senator of Oregon. My word should mean more than that woman's over there." He jabbed his finger in Missy's direction. "She's a nobody."

"On the contrary," Jake said. "She is the daughter of Surgeon John Edgar Douglas, a famous Civil War surgeon, who—I've been told—has been nominated for United States Surgeon General." Murmurs could be heard in the gallery and the judge hammered the gavel to restore order. "I'd say at the moment he outranks you."

"But he's not—" Devlin said.

"No further questions," Jake interrupted. He returned to his seat and stared down at his notes, jotting down a few more. He could feel McCoy's glare on him as he stepped down and returned to the gallery. Jake gazed over at Missy and gave her a wink.

She leaned over to him. "I think you got him very mad."

He whispered back, "Good. That's what I wanted." He raised his hand. "Your Honor, I would like the option of recalling this witness at a later time."

"Granted." The judge pounded his gavel. "We will take an hour recess and reconvene here at twelve hundred hours."

The marshal came over to escort Missy back to jail, but Jake halted him. "I need a word with my client, Marshal."

Marshal Tanner approved.

Jake turned to Missy. "Do you have a lock on your jewelry box?"

She looked utterly confused. "Uh, I think. Why?"

"Could your uncle have put something in there you didn't know about?" he asked.

She shrugged, and then her eyes widened. "He made me that jewelry box. He told me he hand carved it and constructed it especially for me." She placed her hand over Jake's. "He told me several times that I should give the jewelry box to my father the next time I saw him. You don't think—"

"I'm not sure."

"I've got to take her back now," Marshal Tanner said, sounding apologetic.

"When you've returned her to her cell and the deputy is standing guard, meet me at Mrs. Baker's boarding-house," Jake said.

"Why?" Marshal Tanner asked.

"I can't tell you why right now. Can you meet me there?"

"Sure."

Jake stood with Missy. "I've got to check out a few things. The marshal will escort you back to jail. I'll be there as soon as possible." Turning to the crowd that was clearing out of the courtroom, Jake spotted Mrs. Baker. He yelled for her, but she didn't hear him. Taking a side door to the outside, Jake hustled around to the front of the building, searching for the older woman. He couldn't find her anywhere, until he saw her waddling down the hill toward the boardinghouse. Running after her, he caught up. Winded, he said, "I need your help."

She paused and, appearing confused said, "How can I help you?"

"I need to get into Miss Douglas' room again," Jake said.

Mrs. Baker shook her head. "No. I shouldn't have allowed it the first time."

"Miss Douglas would want you to let me in. If you don't believe me, then we can go ask her. But I've only got a short amount of time. Please," he said.

For a stern woman, she also had a soft heart. "Oh, okay." She motioned for him to follow. "Come with me."

They walked at a steady and fast pace down to Jefferson Street. Mrs. Baker opened up the back door and showed Jake up to Missy's room. She pushed wide the bedroom door and stood in the doorway while Jake quickly found the jewelry box.

"You know the day Irvine Douglas was killed he had come here and asked to put something in Missy's room. Missy wasn't here when he came," Mrs. Baker said.

Jake's head darted in her direction. "Why haven't you told me this before?"

"Because the first time you came here I didn't trust you. And—" she shrugged, "—I haven't had the chance to talk to you since you returned to town. Besides, I didn't think it was really that important."

With a surge of hope, Jake picked up the wooden box and set it on the bed. His heart pounded in anticipation. He opened the top of the box as he had done before, and found the solid gold band placed inside. Shutting the top, he turned the box over and examined all four sides, and then the bottom. On one of the bottom edges— there it was—a lock. Jake hadn't noticed the first time he saw the box that it had a false bottom. He pulled the key out of his pocket and slipped it in the lock. The lock clicked open. The bottom of the box slid off and an envelope—a rather thick envelope—dropped out.

Jake glanced at Mrs. Baker, then back to the documents.

"What is it Mr. Gilbert?" Mrs. Baker asked in her Norwegian accent.

"If I told you, you wouldn't believe me," he said. He sank onto the bed and opened the documents. Letters filled with testimonies, along with a photograph of Morgan in his military uniform and Devlin in his street clothes were enclosed. Jake quickly read through the documents, and came upon some damning evidence.

Morgan had the letter C carved on his arm. All the men in his marauding group had them to show what brotherhood they belonged to. The documents also listed other distinguishing features Morgan had such as a pinkie finger with the tip cut off, a scar that ran across his forehead just at the hairline, and scars on his torso from the war wounds he had encountered. Folding the documents back up, he slid them back into the envelope.

"I got him," Jake whispered. He turned to Mrs. Baker. "I need paper." He followed her down to the library where she closed the doors behind them. She gestured to the desk. Jake sat down and scribbled a note to the marshal, and then handed it to her. "Give this to someone reliable and have them take it immediately to the marshal." He grabbed a book off the shelf, ripped pages out of it, folded them, and placed them in a separate envelope. Then he handed the documents to Mrs. Baker. Put this somewhere safe and bring it to the courthouse. I'll pick it up just before court begins at noon.

She looked confused, but agreed.

Jake stuffed the other envelope in his shirt pocket and headed out the door. Only minutes after leaving Mrs. Baker's boardinghouse two men started trailing Jake. One rather large fellow with a small head of bushy black hair, and the other one much shorter and balding. Jake suspected these two worked for McCoy, his two henchmen, Moose and Morty. Halting, Jake turned to confront them.

"In there," Moose said, pointing to an alleyway.

"Speak your mind and be on your way," Jake said.

"You heard the man," Morty said. "In there." He shoved Jake into the alley.

"I'm in the middle of a case, gentlemen," Jake said. "I don't have time for this."

"Make time," Moose said. He thrust a powerful blow to Jake's midsection, doubling him over. Morty followed through with a punch to Jake's jaw, sending him to the ground. Jake tasted the blood from his cracked lip. His teeth felt loose from the impact. He picked himself up slowly.

"Give us the documents," Moose said, or you'll get more of the same.

"I'm not going to give you anything," Jake said. "Did McCoy send you?"

"Yeah," Morty said. "He wanted to say 'howdy.' " He swung at Jake again, but this time Jake blocked the punch and countered with his own powerful swing, connecting to Morty's jaw. The smaller man flew across the alley.

Moose grabbed Jake by the shirt and slammed him into the wood building, nearly knocking the breath from him. "Leave my friend alone."

"You two started this," Jake said, between grunts.

The envelope Jake carried appeared when Moose grabbed his shirt. "Why look here, Morty," Moose said. "Here's the documents right here in his shirt."

"Those are important documents," Jake thrashed. "You cannot take them. My client's life depends on them."

Moose and Morty laughed. Moose stuffed the papers in his own shirt. They both took another punch at Jake before they sauntered out of the alley.

The last punch Moose gave Jake thrust him into the wall, his head whacking against the hard wood. A warm trickle of blood dripped from the side of his forehead.

He slowly stood. His body ached and his head pounded. His jaw felt like the size of a watermelon. Putting one foot in front of the other, he headed out of the alley and for the courthouse.

Along the way Jake received odd stares. When he had nearly reached the courthouse, Dewitt Ireland spotted him and helped him into the building through a back door. "Good Lord what happened to you?" Ireland asked.

"I was attacked along the way," Jake said. "I guess someone in town doesn't like the job I'm doing."

The newspaper reporter gave him a suspicious look. "You promised me an exclusive."

"It's going to be the greatest story of your life," Jake said. "It's going to knock you and your readers' boots off their feet."

Ireland licked his lips in anticipation. "Your attack had something to do with this shocking story?"

"Everything to do with it. And it's all about to unfold in—" Jake checked his pocket watch. "Ten minutes."

"Is there anything I can do to help you?"

"You've done enough. Just let me clean up here." Before Dewitt Ireland left the room Jake said, "Tell Miss Douglas I will be there shortly."

Ireland nodded, and then disappeared around the corner.

Jake stepped over to a table that held a pitcher and basin. Luckily the pitcher was filled with water. He pulled out his handkerchief and cleaned his face. A bruise and swelling had started to form on his lip and forehead. He sucked in a breath when he touched the wet cloth to his cut lip and gouge on his head. He felt a little light-headed as he ambled out of the room. On the way, he tucked his shirt in his trousers, adjusted his tie, and smoothed his jacket, brushing the dirt off it.

By the time Jake reached the courtroom the public and jury had returned and Missy sat at the table alone waiting for him. She gasped, as did many in the audience, when he came in. He imagined the sight he must have made.

Sitting down next to Missy, she grabbed his arm. "What happened?"

"Guess."

"McCoy did this, didn't he?" she said.

"No. His henchmen did. Your friends, Moose and Morty."

She moved his hair to get a better look at his forehead. "I need to tend to this. Can we get the judge to give us a short break?"

Jake shook his head.

"Why did they do this?" Missy asked.

"You'll find out in a moment," Jake said.

The judge took his seat up on the podium and hammered the court into session. He looked at Jake and his eyes widened. "Mr. Gilbert. Would you please approach the bench?"

Murmurs spread throughout the crowd as he stepped up to speak with the judge.

"Mr. Gilbert, what happened to you?"

"A couple of citizens of Astoria didn't agree with what I'm trying to do here," Jake said.

"Are you going to be able to proceed?"

"Yes, Your Honor."

The judge studied him. After a minute of contemplation he said, "Then proceed."

"Thank you, Your Honor." As Jake strolled back to his table, he remained standing. "Your Honor, I would like to recall Mr. Devlin McCoy." While he waited for McCoy to make his journey up to the stand, Jake searched the crowd for Mrs. Baker. Spotting her near the back of the room, he motioned for her to come over to him.

"Do you have the envelope I gave you?" he said.

She nodded. Opening her purse, she pulled it out and handed it to him.

Jake smiled. "I knew I could count on you. I'd kiss you if we weren't in court."

Mrs. Bakers' brows shot up in surprise, and then softened. She grinned, and then returned to her seat.

Jake sat down at the table and opened the documents. All of them were still there, years of Irvine's research. Now, he would do the man justice. He glanced over at Devlin, who wore a confident smile.

"I can't imagine what you want with me now," Devlin said. "I've already testified that Miss Douglas murdered her uncle."

Jake raised his hand, palm out, to silence the man. He stood and strolled over to him. "Mr. McCoy. I just have a few questions to ask you."

"Make it quick," McCoy said. "I've got business to attend to."

"I'm sure you do," Jake said. "Mr. McCoy would you hold your hands out for me and the jury to see."

Devlin frowned. "This is nonsense."

"Your Honor," the prosecutor whined, "this is irrelevant to this case."

"Your Honor," Jake interjected, "I will prove relevance in a minute. It's critical to my case. Please indulge my questioning for a few more minutes?"

Judge Ayers thought for a moment. "Make your point quickly."

"Thank you, Your Honor." Jake turned back to Devlin and the jury. "I notice the tip of your small finger has been cut off."

"So what?"

"Would you roll up your sleeves?"

Devlin grimaced. "Why?"

"Amuse me," Jake said. "Roll up your sleeves."

Devlin hesitated until the judge ordered him to do so.

Jake studied Devlin's right forearm. "You have an old scar on your arm. It looks to be in the shape of the letter C."

Devlin shrugged and immediately slid his sleeves down.

"Now I want you to push the hair back on your forehead." Jake waited. When Devlin did so Jake said to the jury, "I want you to note the scar Mr. McCoy has that follows along his hairline."

Devlin lowered his hand. "What's this all about?"

Jake smiled. "The cut off fingertip, scar on your forearm, and scar along your hairline are all distinguishing characteristics of Colonel James Huge Morgan, the notorious Confederate leader who took his gang and robbed and murdered throughout many northern states.

Devlin paled. "You have no proof."

"You think I have no proof, because you sent your men to beat me up and rob me of documents that would prove who you are," Jake said.

The crowd's murmur rose in volume.

Judge Ayers pounded the gavel, but it took several seconds to gain everyone's attention. "I will remove all of you from the courthouse if you can not control yourselves." The people quieted down. He addressed Jake. "Mr. Gilbert. Proceed, but state your case."

"Yes, Your Honor." Jake strode over to the table where Missy sat, gave her a reassuring smile, and then picked up the documents. "I have an envelope full of documentation that Irvine Douglas had assembled. It was the reason McCoy murdered him and tried to blame it on Miss Melissa Douglas. It took Irvine Douglas years to gain this information, and it is all about Colonel Morgan, who has been parading around as Devlin McCoy for years since the war."

Devlin jumped to his feet. "This is outrageous!" His face, red with anger, was contorted into a hateful sneer. "I'll see you hanged for this."

Jake handed the documents over to the judge. "No, Colonel Morgan. *You* will hang for this and all the heinous crimes you and your men committed."

Devlin yanked out a Colt revolver from the inside of his coat. "I will not go down alone," he said. He vaulted from the witness chair and scurried over to Missy, grabbing her and placing the gun to her head.

Jake watched in horror. He hadn't anticipated this from McCoy. Everyone was supposed to have been checked for weapons before entering the courthouse. He rushed toward them as did Marshal Tanner.

"Back away or she gets it in the head," Devlin said. The two men halted. Devlin backed slowly out the side door, his head twitching side to side, watching the audience closely.

Missy's heart pounded like a hammer in her chest. She felt the cold steel pressing against her temple and knew one false move and McCoy would pull the trigger. She hated this man. He had killed her uncle, and she was determined not to let him kill two Douglases.

Once they backed out of the courtroom, he faced her forward in front of him jabbing the gun into her back. "Get out of my way," Devlin yelled. The crowd separated, letting them through, but many of the women and children screamed and ran.

Missy paused at a horse and carriage and Devlin said, "Get in and drive us down to the docks." She climbed in and Devlin followed on her heels. Missy snapped the reins on the horse's back.

Devlin placed one arm around her back, while he pointed the gun at her with his other hand. "Hurry it up."

Missy had no idea if Jake was following them or not. She thought maybe the marshal was, but didn't dare glance behind to find out. Her hands shook as she held the reins. From the corner of her eye she could see the barrel of the revolver staring at her.

"If that damn bounty hunter hadn't failed, both of you would be out of my hair, and I would have been the next senator of Oregon. Damn you both. Damn you to hell."

"I think the only one going to hell here is you," Missy said.

He smacked her on the back of the head. The impact left a ringing sound in Missy's head.

They reached the dock where a pilot boat sat ready

for Devlin, undoubtedly his backup plan. Moose and Morty were already on board. Missy realized she would be dead within seconds once she stepped foot on board.

As soon as the carriage stopped, Devlin grabbed Missy by the arm and yanked her out behind him. She fell to the ground, but Devlin never let go of her. Her arm felt as if it had been wrenched from its socket.

"Get up," he demanded.

"I'm trying to," she said. Missy took her time. Many people had followed them down to the docks, but all of them, including the marshal and Jake kept their distance. She realized it was up to her to save her own life. As they neared the gangway, Missy knew what she had to do.

"You first," Devlin said. He shoved her onto the gangplank. She stumbled forward. Then without warning, she fell into the water. The minute she hit the icy Columbia her lungs froze. Underwater, she heard muted sounds of the gun going off and had no doubt McCoy was shooting at her.

She swam directly under the piers where it would be hard for McCoy to get a direct line of fire. The weight of her skirt began to pull her down. She grabbed for one of the pilings to hold her up, but struggled. The cold temperatures of the water had frozen her hands so they barely moved. She treaded water, but knew she would not hold out long.

More gunfire erupted from somewhere above her. She wasn't even sure she was being fired at any longer or not. Then as quickly as it had started, the gun play ended. Missy heard a splash from the side of the dock.

Surfacing, Jake called, "Missy!" He dove under the water.

When he came up she called, "Jake. I'm over here."

With brisk strokes, he swam over to her and grabbed her, holding her tight while he treaded water. "I thought I'd lost you." With his good arm around her, he used his wounded one to paddle them to the docks. Many people waited there to help them up. Once on the dock, Mrs. Baker draped wool blankets around them.

The crowd cheered.

Jake gripped Missy's blanket and pulled her into him. He kissed her, deeply. But the kiss did not last long, to Missy's disappointment. People patted them on the back and congratulated Jake for a job well done.

Ireland came up to them. "I get an exclusive. Don't forget."

Jake nodded. "I told you it would knock your socks off."

Richard pushed through the crowd until he reached Missy. He plucked her from Jake's grip and held her in a tight hug. "My dear Missy. You've been through such an ordeal. Are you okay?"

"I'm fine," Missy said.

He turned to Jake, but instead of insulting him he said, "I owe you a debt of gratitude. I might have misjudged you." He shook Jake's hand.

"Come now," Mrs. Baker said. "Let's get you two into a warm house, dried off, and get warm food in your bellies."

Jake kissed Mrs. Baker on the cheek. The older woman blushed. "I owe you one," Jake said.

"I didn't do much," she mumbled. "I didn't even know what I was carrying with me."

The sheriff shoved Devlin forward, his hands tied

behind his back. Devlin paused next to Jake. Blood oozed from the arm he held. Sneering at Jake, he said, "Some friend you turned out to be."

"I told you you didn't want me as your enemy," Jake said.

"My only regret is that I didn't hire a better assassin to kill you," Devlin said. "If I had I'd be the next senator of Oregon."

"Better save that for hell, Morgan, because that's where you're going after they hang you for your crimes."

"Well, I guess someday I'll see you there." Devlin grinned.

Sheriff Tanner pushed McCoy to get him to break the stare he was holding with Jake and get him moving forward, headed for the jailhouse.

"Now I know why I never liked you, McCoy," Marshall Tanner said. "Guess my instincts were right about you."

After they moved on, Mrs. Baker ushered Missy and Jake back to her boardinghouse where they took warm baths, changed into dry clothing, and ate warm food.

During the next few days, Jake went over the documents with the judge, notified the military, and gave the newspaper reporter an exclusive interview. Mr. Ireland made sure newspapers all over the country ran the article, which made Jake appear like a national hero, having uncovered the notorious Col. James Huge Morgan. Mr. Ireland had told him that Jake had redeemed himself. Jake realized he no longer needed to feel guilty. Robert Jackson had murdered Rachael. Jake had only loved her. He knew Rachael's father would go to his grave always blaming Jake for the death of his daughter, but Jake also realized that her father and her family needed someone to blame. He had been that someone.

But no longer.

Devlin McCoy was turned over to the military along with the incriminating documents. An expert was coming out to officially identify him, but everyone knew Jake had already done that in court. As for Moose and Morty, they would stand trial for their part in McCoy's schemes.

Jake strolled from the Occident Hotel over to Mrs. Baker's boardinghouse, where Missy was staying. He asked to meet with her in the parlor. He had something very important to talk to her about.

She came in wearing a blue dress and her hair pulled back in a bun. The black bags and worried lines under and around her eyes had disappeared, leaving her looking rested and refreshed. She had never looked more beautiful to him than she did at this moment, which made what he had to say to her all the harder. When she smiled at him he held his breath.

He resisted the temptation to pull her into his arms and savor her lips possibly one last time. "Missy," Jake began, "I know we had an agreement between us, and I've decided I will no longer hold you to that agreement. You don't have to marry me."

She tilted her head back as if he had slapped her in the face. Tears filled her eyes. In a whisper, she said, "You don't want to marry me?"

"Of course I want to marry you," he said. "I just don't want you to marry me out of gratitude." He took her hands into his and gazed into her eyes. "I want your heart."

She released a sharp breath. "Don't you know you've had it since the day we met?"

Jake's heart filled with joy. Did he hear her right? He knelt on one knee and gazed up at her. "Melissa Douglas. May I have your hand in marriage?"

She placed her hands on either side of his face. "Yes. Yes. Yes," she said.

Jake grinned, stood, and kissed her. He decided her lips were indeed sweeter than the apple after all.

Epilogue

Jake stood outside the church waiting for the ceremony to take place in another hour. He rolled and lit a cigarette, smoking it to calm his nerves. "How do you do, sir?" Jake said.

Melissa's father slapped Jake on the shoulder. "Don't call me sir. Don't you dare call me Surgeon Douglas. Call me John. You're marrying my little girl. Family shouldn't be formal with one another."

Jake had expected her father to be much more rigid than he was, after what Missy had said about him. Perhaps moving into the political arena had taught him to be more relaxed and open with people.

"Shouldn't we be smoking cigars?" John asked, and then lit one up.

"I don't smoke very often," Jake said, "only when I'm nervous."

"Hell I was so nervous before I got married I smoked

enough cigars to send up Indian smoke signals," John said, and then laughed.

"Don't get me wrong," Jake said, "I love your daughter and want to marry her more than I've wanted anything in my life. It's just—"

"It's just that marriage is a scary thing," John said. "I know what you mean, son."

"I want to make Missy happy."

"And you will, Jake." John sobered, his graying bushy brows drawing together. "There is one thing I wanted to talk to you about, though."

"What's that?"

"Your past."

Jake fell silent. Here he went again. When would his past stop haunting him? "So you know about my past," Jake said. "And you're going to tell me not to marry your daughter because of it."

The doctor frowned. "Hell, no. I was going to tell you that I thought you were one of the best damn lawyers I'd ever seen. You were wronged, Jake. I think Hancock ran you out of town because he was afraid of you." He took a drag on his cigar. "I bet you didn't hear that shortly after you left town Thomas Hancock had a total breakdown and ended up in an insane asylum."

The news shocked Jake. He hadn't heard any of this. "I wasn't aware of that," Jake said.

"Let me tell you, son. Had I been here when Missy had been in trouble with this McCoy fellow, you would have been the first one I hired to defend her."

"That's good to hear," Jake said, feeling a huge sense of relief.

"You two put those smelly things out," said Missy's mother Sarah as she joined them. "People are coming and the minister needs to speak with both of you before the ceremony begins."

"Yes, dear," John said, snuffing out his cigar.

Jake dropped his cigarette on the ground and stepped on it with the toe of his shoe. "I guess we had better go."

"One more thing, Jake," John said. "Forget about your past, because all that matters is your future with my daughter, and your future as a lawyer. Uncovering Colonel Morgan has made you famous once again. Go forward in life, learn from your past, and then never look back."

Jake smiled. "I'll do that."

As the ceremony began Jake watched Missy join him at the front of the church. All the people who had supported him came to celebrate their union. Mrs. Baker and Mrs. O'Sullivan sat together dabbing their eyes, DeWitt Ireland was there with his notepad and pencil in hand, Private Tom Pickering gave him the thumbs up, and Simon stood by his side as his best man. Even Surgeon Richard Barnes was there giving them his blessing, having also promised to marry the mother of his son and give his son a proper name.

His soon-to-be father-in-law's words rang in his ear. "Go forward in life and never look back." Jake realized that with Missy by his side he could finally let go of the past and have a life full of love. No longer would he live alone. No longer would he look for traces of love, because he had finally found the entire heart-filled track.